I hope you're doing okay x

THANK YOU FOR READING this book, I really, truly hope Maureen's Song makes you smile. I loved writing it! As well as the Guesthouse on the Green series I've written eight standalone novels—they're all written with humour and warmth and I like to think, if you read my books, they'll make you feel you're curling up with friends for a cosy chat. If you enjoy Maureen's Song then taking the time to say so by leaving a review would be wonderful. A book review is the best present you can give an author. If you'd like to hear about my new releases, you can subscribe to my Newsletter by visiting my website at www.michellevernalbooks.com[1] and to say thank you, you'll receive an exclusive O'Mara women character profile!- Take care xx

---

1. http://www.michellevernalbooks.com

Also by Michelle Vernal

Michelle Vernal asserts the moral right to be identified as the author of this work.

This novel, Maureen's Song is entirely a work of fiction. The names, characters and incidents portrayed in it are the work of the author's imagination. Any resemblance to actual persons, living or dead, events or localities is entirely coincidental.

Maureen's Song
by
Michelle Vernal

Chapter 1

Dublin 2000

MAUREEN O'MARA STARED into her bathroom mirror trying to be objective. Was the face reflected back at her the sorta face you'd want to kiss? Not a peck on the cheek kiss either, a proper kiss on the lips. She wasn't too bad, she thought, angling her head so she only had the one chin and smiling the way she'd done for Aisling's wedding photos. This pose was a hot tip she'd received from Marian who belonged to her rambling group. Marian had brought some pictures in to show the group, of her daughter Amy's big day and while she'd looked as though she might have been sending a prayer to Him up there in most of the photos, Marian did not have so much as a whiff of a double chin. When it came to the business of having your photo taken once you were a certain age you had to decide what mattered more—looking as if you were saying a prayer or having an all-in-one chin-neck. Mind, if Aisling had been marrying a chap with a face the sea wouldn't even give a wave to like Marian's poor daughter, she'd have been looking heavenward too.

In the end, Maureen had found a happy medium and the feedback when she'd passed the photographs she'd had taken on her camera so as she didn't have to wait for Aisling to sort the official wedding photographs out, was positive. The ramblers on the whole agreed she had a mysterious air peering out from under her hat, like so, which was exactly the look she'd been going for and there'd been no mention of chin-necks or prayers.

Maureen wiped the fog her breath had caused from the mirror and held her head straight, looking at her reflection square on. She placed her fingertips on the top of both cheek-bones and pulled her skin back to see what she'd look like if she was one of those Los Angeles types. Sure, even the men were at it over there because she'd an inkling her dear departed Brian's brother, Cormac had been under the knife. It was likely only a little nip and tuck but he'd been looking very smooth and stretched when he'd been over for Aisling's wedding, and Maureen had spent a great deal of time trying to spot a telltale scar behind his ears. Several of the ramblers had asked who he was when they'd seen the wedding photographs and when she'd mentioned he was Brian's older brother they'd gasped and said, 'Never!' As for the other man in her life over in Los Angeles, her first born and only son Patrick, his teeth had made her want to sing *Blinded by the Light* every time he smiled this last visit. The bride was supposed to be centre of attention at a wedding not a set of gleaming, white teeth.

She put Patrick's obsessive dentistry down to the sunshine and oranges; too much sunshine and vitamin C wasn't good for an Irishman. His American girlfriend Cindy wasn't a good influence either because her teeth were the same, like piano keys they were. In fact, she wouldn't be surprised if they got a two for one deal at the dentist. Like distant relatives of the Osmond family the pair of them were these days. Marie and Donny's lost-lost cousins. Then there were the two enormous watermelons attached to Cindy's chest. They were far too perky to be the set the good Lord saw fit to bless her with and Patrick could do with taking a leaf out of Marian's book and looking up where his girlfriend was concerned. He always had his nose near the things.

His girlfriend bore an uncanny resemblance to the Barbie dolls the girls had played with when they were young. Come to think of it, she'd caught Patrick doing something untoward with his Ken doll to Rosi's Barbie once. Rosi had been most put out and she'd snapped Ken's leg off. Oh, the drama of it all. She could still hear them shrieking and calling each other all the names under the sun. Perhaps that's where his penchant for blonde women with big bosoms stemmed from. She didn't want to think about Patrick, though. Not right now.

Her mind flitted in that direction anyway. Ten thousand American dollars she'd loaned him at Christmas and not a word from him about it since. There'd been no time to ask him how his new venture was going when he'd been over for the wedding because he'd been gone again in the blink of an eye. She'd have liked to have known the money had gone to good use and things were going well for him. It would have given her some peace if he'd at least acknowledged the loan and reassured her it would be repaid before the year was out. Then, she might not be feeling uneasy about the whole thing. She hated to think what Rosi, Aisling and Moira would say if they knew. No doubt it would be colourful!

The problem was she only had the one son and the last time she'd not done what he wanted which was sell the family guest-house and split the proceeds amongst them all, she'd not heard from him for a good while. He'd flounced off to Los Angeles and look what had happened to him since then. He was in *therapy* he'd confided on this last trip home. Now that was an

American thing, if ever she'd heard one. What did a boy with his looks and charisma need with therapy? And if he had a few things he wanted to get off his chest then what was wrong with going down to St Theresa's, sitting in the confessional box, and talking it out with Father Fitzpatrick? It was free for one thing and you went home with a clear conscience to boot.

No, you got to a certain age in life when you realised what was important and family was everything. You didn't want to be at odds with them, not when you knew how quickly they could be taken from you. There was Brian, fighting fit one minute and in the ground six months later. He wouldn't have approved of her parting with their hard-earned money like so either. He'd taken a tougher line with Patrick which was why their son would come to her on the quiet with his woes. Family had to help one another, she liked to say, but the niggly voice in her head would override it with, 'That's all fine and dandy, Maureen, but a woman of your years can't be throwing her money around, either.'

She realised she was still stretching her face in a manner that would have had her saying to the girls, 'The wind will change and you'll be stuck like that.' She inspected this new look and decided she looked like your German cat woman, the one who'd been married to a trillionaire. Her photo was always in the magazines beside captions saying *Why you shouldn't have a facelift*. Yer woman had more money than sense and given she could afford the best in the business what hope was there for the rest of them? If she went under the knife, she'd likely wind up looking like the old bint over the way's Persian cat, Peaches. It had a face on it like a smacked arse and had taken to taunting Pooh. The ball of fluff liked nothing better than to peer around their adjoining balcony rails and stare in at her poor poodle like some sort of cat-demon. The first time she'd seen the ball of fluff there, she'd taken fright thinking it was one of those furry things from the *Star Wars* films. She dropped her hands to her side and let everything fall back into place.

Donal had said she was a fine-looking woman when he'd flicked through the wedding photos and he'd looked over at her with a gleam in his eyes. It was a gleam she'd not seen in a good long while, not since Brian, but she still recognised it. The gleam told her he'd like to kiss her. Now, she puckered her lips and half closed her eyes homing in on her reflection. Jaysus wept! The poor man would take fright with that coming at him, she thought, opening her eyes and stepping back from the mirror. There was a whining and scrabbling at the door. She'd been in here long enough. It was time she took Pooh for a walk.

She opened the door with a sigh, knowing she'd find the poodle sitting with his lead in his mouth right outside it to be certain she didn't miss him. The first time he'd plonked himself there she'd nearly gone over and, there but for the grace of God, she could have wound up needing her hip replaced like Rosemary Farrell. She'd copped on to his tricks now. 'Let me get my coat on and we'll see what the day's doing out there.' He stood up and ruffed. Maureen scratched behind his ear. 'It's all very hard this business of meeting someone new when you've been a married woman since you were a girl of twenty, you know, Pooh, and you don't help.'

The poodle had a bad attitude when it came to Donal. He was jealous and Maureen had hoped he'd get over this if Donal joined them for his obedience classes but he'd been very disobedient at the last one. He was a tolerant man, was Donal.

There weren't many men who'd put up with being bitten on the arse by a green-eyed, standard poodle and having to have a tetanus shot as a result.

The instructor had said she was going to have to keep a watchful eye on Pooh's behaviour around Donal. Maureen had rebutted, she wasn't paying good money to be told the obvious, and the instructor had puffed up like one of those strange Japanese fish she'd seen on a nature programme before advising her distraction and reward was key when it came to cultivating obedient behaviour. She was to distract the poodle when he began to tense and growl in Donal's presence and reward him when he behaved calmly. Lots of positive reinforcement was needed. This was something she was dubious about because she'd been told to do the same thing with Moira when she was a troublesome teenager. It hadn't worked. What *had* worked was telling her, 'I brought you into this world, my girl, and I can take you out just as easily.' Usually followed by a wave of the wooden spoon.

So, here she was having to walk around with a packet of doggy treats in her coat pocket at all times. Sure, she'd been like the Pied Piper of Howth Harbour in a red coat the other day as she'd set off down the pier with an entourage of cocker spaniel, Labrador and feisty Dalmatian in tow.

Pooh looked up at her now with his head cocked to one side. 'You're not going to make me choose you know. So, you might as well accept that Donal's going to be a part of my life. Just like the girls are going to have to do the same. I'm seeing him tonight for your information. We're going out for dinner.'

Pooh whined.

'And it's no good whining, so cop on to yourself.' She retrieved her coat from where it was hanging in the utility room.' Pooh padded after her wanting guarantees she wasn't going to get sidetracked by an afternoon episode of *Emmerdale* or the like. 'There's no one I can talk to about Donal either, except you,' she said to him as she slid into the red parker and zipped it up. 'I'm not the girl who sat giggling with her friends over the peck she'd fended off from Beanpole Brown anymore. He tried his luck after taking me to the cinema, you know. I'm a widowed woman, Pooh, of a pensionable age so I am.' She headed toward the front door. 'I don't have those sort of conversations with Rosemary or Marian or my golfing girls and I certainly couldn't have them with Rosi, Aisling or Moira.' The thought of the look on any of their faces were she to ask their advice as to what she should do when Donal tried to have his way with her made her chortle. 'So, you're it,' she said, venturing out and shutting the door behind them.

Chapter 2

THE RESTAURANT DONAL had booked them into was an Italian place in Raheny which had been garnering good reviews. It was halfway between where he lived in Drumcondra and where she lived in Howth. Maureen insisted on driving herself to meet him even though he'd offered to pick her up. It would have made for a long round trip and she was worried it'd be painful for him to sit for so long. Pooh's poodly teeth were sharp and had indeed made their mark. She hadn't wanted to risk another encounter between them just yet either. Not until she felt she was making headway with this positive reinforcement doggy treat business.

It wasn't the best night to be out and about, she thought, hunching over the steering wheel as the windscreen wipers worked overtime. She could feel her little car getting buffeted at the lights but she managed to find the bistro without too much trouble and was grateful for the easy car parking behind the restaurant. It was not the night to be walking miles. The car slid into a space and she locked it before wrapping her coat around her and walking briskly to the entrance of Amalfi's. That the restaurant was dimly lit registered first as she stepped inside. This was a worry, insomuch as Rosemary Farrell had gotten a bout of food poisoning from a Mexican place she'd gone to with her daughter. It too had been dimly lit and Rosemary was adamant the lack of lighting was to hide the lack of hygiene.

Maureen gave a tentative sniff. It certainly smelt appetising and not at all like the sorta place where cockroaches would be lurking, she decided, inhaling the warm, yeasty aroma of pizza dough.

Her coat was whisked away by the maître d' who lacked the flamboyant welcome she so enjoyed whenever she frequented, Aisling's Quinn's bistro. She was introduced to their waiter for the evening, who was about as Italian as she was with his red hair and freckles. His name, he said, in broad Dublin tones, was Antony. She fancied he'd made that up and his real name was Seamus, which suited him much better, as he led her over to the table where Donal was already seated. She put a hand up to her hair hoping the biting wind hadn't undone all her hard work with the hairdryer earlier. She was aiming for a soft wave not a Farrah Fawcett flick.

Donal was old-school in the manners' department, like Brian had been, and he stood up seeing her approach. His bearded face broke into a smile and his eyes lit up in a way that made her feel special. She turned her cheek and his lips, soft and warm, brushed her skin, his beard tickling her and giving her goosebumps—the good kind. He was looking very handsome in a white shirt and navy trousers. The crisp line down the middle of each leg didn't escape her notice and the thought of him thinking she was worth the effort of ironing them pleased her.

'Maureen O'Mara you look a picture, and you smell wonderful. Tell me again what your perfume's, called,' he boomed, and Maureen saw a few heads turn their way. Donal didn't give a flying toss what others thought of him and she admired this quality amongst others in him.

'Arpège,' she said, straightening her dress and feeling pleased she'd taken the young girl's, who needed a good meal inside of her, advice. It was what was called a wrap style.

'It's very flattering around here,' the girl in the Howth boutique whose window display she often admired when walking Pooh, had said, patting her own non-existent midriff. Outside a plaintive whining had begun and Maureen had had to excuse herself in order to tell Pooh to quieten down or he'd be getting none of the treats she had in her pocket because his behaviour wasn't falling into the positive reward realm.

'I've had four children, you know, and one of them was over ten pounds,' Maureen replied on her return, patting her own middle. 'So, think on—'

'Ciara, and I've no plans for children. I'm too young.'

'Or lunch or dinner either, by the looks of you.'

'I'm naturally thin.'

Maureen didn't trust anyone who was naturally thin so when Ciara held up a dress and said, 'Well now, this will be perfect for you then. It will streamline you where you need it.' She'd been sceptical even when Ciara had taken a big sucky-in breath to demonstrate where Maureen needed streamlining.

'I can see your ribs, young lady. Does your mammy not make you breakfast?'

'Oh, I don't do breakfast. I'm a coffee on the go, girl.'

'Well I'm a mammy and I say you need to eat your breakfast. It's the most important meal of the day and there's a bakery next door where you could get yourself a nice egg sandwich for your lunch, too.'

Donal interrupted her reverie. 'I've not seen you in that colour before, it's lovely on you,' he said, waiting for her to sit down.

'Thank you.' Maureen smiled as Antony held her chair out for her. Electric blue wasn't normally a colour she'd wear but Ciara had assured her it looked well on her. She'd felt like living dangerously and so she'd splurged, on the condition Ciara got herself a sandwich from next door for her lunch and ate a bowl of porridge before she left for work the next morning. They'd shaken on it.

Maureen sat down and Donal did the same. The waiter flapped around with her napkin and she resisted snatching it from him and telling him not to be making such a performance of things. It was an oversized hanky to be placed on the diner's lap, not a rug you were after beating.

'I hope you're hungry?' Donal beamed as he was handed the drinks menu. He pulled his reading glasses from his shirt pocket and inspected the list.

'I am, it smells wonderful in here.' Maureen beamed back. 'Very garlicky.'

Donal knew she was partial to a red and he knew a thing or two about wine because he'd done a night school class on wine tasting so Maureen was happy to sit back and let him order. They agreed a garlic bread to share as a starter would be lovely.

'How's your erm...' she lowered her eyes to the red chequered cloth covering the table, the candle flickering between them casting shadowy light across it.

'Grand, there's only a bit bruising there now.'

'He's very sorry, you know.'

Donal laughed that rumbly belly laugh of his. 'I'm sure he is.' It was said in a tone that said he didn't believe a word of it. 'You know, Maureen, I had a punch in the nose from the fella my Ida was courting before me for making eyes at her when I was a young fellow but a bite on the arse from a jealous poodle, well I have to say that's a first.'

Most of the restaurant's patrons looked their way upon hearing this. They went back to their meals when Maureen began to chatter about her day. 'I had a lazy morning catching up on my chores followed by a spot of shopping and then this afternoon I went to my watercolour painting class after which I took Pooh for a walk down the pier.' She'd not be mentioning the ten minutes or so of stargazing at her own face she'd done in the bathroom mirror trying to see herself through Donal's eyes.

'How's the self-portrait coming along?'

'Grand.' Maureen was pleased with it. She felt she'd captured her essence and yes, so what if she'd shaved a few years off and given herself a lovely big head of hair like her favourite actress from *Ballykissangel*, Dervla Kirwan. Better that than the modernistic style Rosemary Farrell was after painting. She said it was reminiscent of Picasso's style only in watercolour and she thought she might give it to her daughter who had a big birthday coming up. Maureen thought it might finish her off, poor love, ripping off the paper and being confronted by a face that would drive rats from the barn, but she'd kept that to herself.

'I hope it's going to be hanging on my wall.'

Maureen giggled. 'Ah, you don't want me looking down at you from your wall when you're trying to watch the tele.'

'I wouldn't mind having you keep an eye on me.' His grey eyes danced.

She blushed and was grateful for the flickering candlelight as she changed the subject. 'I had a postcard from Aisling today. She wrote that she and Quinn are having a whale of a time over there in Sweden, only she doesn't write it like that. Every sentence starts with 'my husband and I' like she's the Queen.'

'Newlyweds.' Donal commented with a smile.

Maureen smiled back, acutely aware of his knee resting against hers under the table. 'They've seen the Northern Lights and fed Reindeer. They've even been on a sleigh ride pulled by doggies.'

'Huskies.'

Maureen nodded and then frowned. 'I still don't know why you'd want to have your honeymoon somewhere you'd have to wear more layers than an onion has skins but my girls always have to rub against the grain.'

Donal winked. 'I'm sure they're finding plenty of ways to keep themselves warm.'

Maureen's face grew hot in a way it hadn't since she'd gone through the menopause. She could have done with the big fan she'd carried around with her for the best part of a year, like a genteel lady from Victorian times, now, to hide coquettishly behind. Only back then there'd been nothing genteel about the way she used to rattle the bottle of Vitamin B6 tablets her doctor had prescribed to settle her hormones whenever someone in the family was annoying. It was a warning to them they were entering into what she called the danger zone. All that rattling and fan beating had been very exhausting.

She was saved from having to answer by the arrival of the wine. It was a rich, ruby red colour which Donal assured her after going through the palaver of swirling and then tasting the tiddly amount Antony poured into the bottom of his glass, was a warm, oaky flavour. 'That will do nicely,' he said, and when their glasses had been filled and Antony had disappeared, he turned his attention to Maureen. 'Now then, I wanted to talk to you about a luncheon date for when your Aisling and Quinn are home and have got their breath back. What do you think to us going to Johnnie Fox's over there in Wicklow; the seafood's very good I hear?'

Maureen sat up straighter in her chair. 'Oh, look here comes the garlic bread.' It was only a temporary diversion she knew but it would give her the chance to gather her thoughts because she knew what was coming next.

The herby, buttered bread was placed in front of them and they each helped themselves, taking a bite while it was steaming hot.

Donal waggled what was left of his loaf in Maureen's direction. 'As I was saying. What do you think to Johnnie Fox's? I'd very much like our two families to meet. I feel as though I'm sneaking around behind their backs and I'm too old for that sort of carry on. I'm very proud to be seen out and about with you, Maureen, and I don't want to have to make excuses to my girls as to where I'm going and what I'm doing any longer.'

It was the most masterful she'd heard Donal sound and her legs went weak under the table. He reminded her of Daniel Day Lewis in her favourite role of his *Last of the Mohicans* only with the look of Kenny Rogers about him. She quashed the image of Donal rampaging through the Irish countryside in a loin

cloth and concentrated on her garlic bread so as she didn't have
to meet his eyes.

Donal had told her his girls. Louise and Anna had taken
to ringing him constantly since Ida had passed despite having
busy lives of their own to be paying attention to. She'd had a
heart attack at the wheel of her car and mercifully nobody else
had been killed but it had come as such shock to them all losing her all of a sudden. Even now, four years later, his daughters
wanted to know where their dad was and what he was doing, in
case. He'd told them his heart was perfectly fine and he wasn't
going anywhere but their sense of security had died along with
their mother. It was a sad state of affairs and if he was learning
to live again then they needed to learn to do so too. 'They like
to think they're looking after me the way their mother would
have wanted them to but Ida would have wanted me to get
on with things and she certainly wouldn't have wanted me to
be reliant on our children.' Maureen had listened carefully to
what he'd said and come back with the reply that children never see their parents as adults with needs and wants of their own.
'They're Mum or they're Dad plain and simple, she'd said.

'So, Maureen, lunch?' Donal pressed once more.

There was no getting out of it. Maureen could tell by his
serious expression she'd not be able to stall or skirt around the
edges of what he was asking. She put her bread down and rest-
ed both hands on the table, her wedding ring glinting under the
light. He was right, she knew he was. The girls had begun making wisecracks that she was stepping out with Liam Finnegan,
yer man missing his two front teeth who busked on Grafton
Street by whistling Irish Rovers hits through the gap. How
everybody knew his name, Maureen didn't know, but they did.

He'd probably been in the papers at some point in time but either way the joke was wearing thin because every time she'd seen Moira of late, she'd taken to whistling *My Old Man's a Dustman* just to annoy her. She was far too smart for her own good that one.

'Johnnie Fox's for lunch it is. Sure, the craic's mighty there.' The atmosphere in the well- known pub would be good even if it was frosty at their table.

Donal was pleased. 'I'm sure they'll all get along great guns.'

Maureen wished she had his confidence.

'I'm partial to lasagne myself what about you?'

'I like the sound of the ravioli, Donal.'

They ordered their main course and while they waited for their food, Donal told her about a gig he had coming up at the end of the month. His Kenny Rogers tribute band, The Gamblers would be playing at a seventieth birthday bash in Clontarf. 'The birthday girl's favourite songs are *Islands in the Stream* and *We've got Tonight* which don't sound the same with fat Davey doing the duet. Maureen, can you perchance sing?'

'I can hold a tune.'

'How do you feel about being Dolly and Sheena to my Kenny?'

'Oh, I don't know, Donal.' Maureen hadn't expected that and her mind was racing. She'd thoroughly enjoyed herself at Aisling's hen night doing the karaoke, skirt tucked into her knickers aside. Everybody had said she'd been very entertaining.

'The band needs you. I need you.'

Well now, she could hardly say no to that, now could she?

Chapter 3

MAUREEN PUT A TEASPOON of bicarbonate soda into the glass and poured warm water on it. It fizzed up like a mini volcano and when it had finished hissing and spitting, she drank it down, banging the glass down on the worktop like a tequila slammer. Not that she'd ever drink tequila again, not after Aisling's hen night. She caught sight of her grimacing face in the reflection of the kitchen window as she swallowed the bitter tonic. It was horrid but it would save the tiramisu she'd shared with Donal against her better judgement, coming back to haunt her in the wee hours. She never slept well when she partook of too much rich food. There was another reason she didn't think she'd sleep well and that was because for the first time in a very long while she'd been kissed. Properly kissed.

Her index finger went to her lips and she smiled to herself, staring into the inkiness outside. Donal had settled the bill despite her protestations that she was a modern woman and, in the end, they'd agreed that she would treat him to that new Tom Hanks film everybody was raving about, *Cast Off* on Thursday. Would they sit in the back row of the cinema and would his arm slide around the back of the seat before he kissed her in the cinema like they were young ones? It was how he was making her feel, like a young girl who was experiencing flutterings in places she'd thought had long since stopped beating their wings. Donal McCarthy had put a spring in her step and brought a glow to her skin. He was better than any youth elixir or fancy serum, Moira was so fond of.

They'd wandered out into that fierce weather and he'd wrapped his strong arm around her, protecting her from the elements. Her coat had flapped around her calves as they'd made their way around the back of the restaurant to where they'd parked. She wasn't in a hurry this time because she liked the solid weight of his arm around her and the warmth she could feel of his body as their coats rubbed against each other. They'd stopped beside her car and Donal had turned her gently toward him. There'd been no time to ponder what she should do and she'd instinctively closed her eyes and tilted her head back, losing herself in the sensation of his warm, soft lips on hers. It had been gentle, searching, tender and yes, there'd been the promise of something else to come in that kiss, but not yet. She hadn't wanted it to end but the burst of laughter and sudden flash of light as one of the kitchen hands stepped out of the back door of the building to cart a bag of rubbish over to the bins saw them break apart.

'I'd best be getting home then.' Maureen had fumbled in her pocket for her keys and, locating them, she aimed them at her car.

'Maureen...'

'Yes?'

'You're a special woman, so you are, and I'm very glad to have met you.'

She'd given him a smile as she opened her door. 'I'm glad I've met you too.'

They'd grinned at one another like idiots until a car door slamming on the street broke the spell. 'Goodnight, Donal.'

She'd gotten in her car, gunning it into life and she'd driven home with an enormous smile plastered to her face. It hadn't faltered, not even when some eejit had failed to stop on the orange light, an act that would have normally had her hand pressing on the horn and fantasising about citizens' arrests.

This time it was Pooh who broke her trance by positioning himself at her feet before stretching a paw up to rest on either side of her blue wrap dress, which triggered the response he'd been aiming for. There was no such thing as bad attention in his opinion, attention was attention and he'd been home alone all evening. He'd entertained himself with a game of peekaboo with Peaches next door before having a one-sided battle with his rubber bone. Then he'd settled down to listen to the Kenny Roger's CD Maureen had left playing before having a ribald game with his ball. Now, he was ready for a pat, snack and bed. In that order, thank you very much. He planned on plonking himself at the foot of Maureen's bed tonight where the nice soft blanket she kept folded over was because he should be given special dispensation to the 'in your basket' rule on account of her being out all evening.

Maureen poured some dry food in his bowl and as she padded toward her room spied the blinking light of the answerphone. She sighed, pushing play in case it was urgent.

'Mammy, it's Moira. Where are you? It's Tuesday night. Nobody goes out on a Tuesday night. I wanted to see what you thought to Carol Foley falling off the wagon but you're not home.' There was click as she hung up. It took Maureen a second to realise Moira was talking about Carol from *Fair City* the Dublin soap opera neither of them would hold their hands up to being addicted to. She glanced over at the tele. She'd recorded it but now she knew what happened there was no point in watching it. Tom must have been waiting tables at Quinn's tonight, or studying, because she wouldn't have telephoned her mammy, unless she was home by herself. It was becoming clear to Maureen that while her girls were all entitled to be caught up with their fellas, they'd grown used to Maureen being on her own. Sure, she was a hard woman to pin down during the day because she'd kept herself busy by joining all manner of community groups since she'd moved to Howth but the evenings had stretched long. The thing was she hadn't ever lived on her own before.

Maureen had grown up in a small cottage in the village of Ballyclegg. There'd been seven of them squeezed inside its stone walls. And while it hadn't been the happiest of childhoods there'd always been comings and goings. She'd left that cottage for Dublin and not looked back as soon as she was able and had found work at O'Mara's guesthouse where she'd met Brian whose mammy and daddy ran the place. She'd had to leave Dublin in order to show him how much he'd miss her and had gone adventuring to Liverpool where she'd lived in a lodging house. There'd always been doors banging shut, taps groaning and shouts from the street below. Mrs Murphy, the landlady, could always be found in the kitchen with the kettle waiting to be boiled, keen to hear all about Maureen's day.

The sounds of life had always carried on around her but here in her double glazed, insulated apartment, the only sound was that of the radio or the television. It had helped when she'd wound up with Pooh but still it wasn't the same because he could hardly make her a cup of tea and ask her how her afternoon had been. He didn't sit opposite her at the table and share a meal or help with the washing-up. She wasn't the sort of mammy to moan either. She didn't tell Rosi, Aisling or Moira how alone she'd felt these last few years because they'd only have turned around and said, 'But you're not alone, Mammy. You've got us.'

She wouldn't think about how they'd take to Donal either. No, tonight she'd remember the way Donal's lips had felt against hers. She felt Brian's eyes boring into her then and she marched up to his photograph. 'And don't you be looking at me like that. It doesn't mean I love you any less. You were my sun and moon, Brian O'Mara, but you're not here anymore and it's been a lonely life without you.' She picked up the photo and carried it through to her room. 'How did you get in here so fast you naughty boy?'

Pooh was already ensconced on the bed. He'd curled up into a ball of curls and was pretending to be asleep. He was too big as a standard poodle for Maureen to lift and so she placed Brian's photograph on the bedside table before doing her ablutions. She climbed into bed weary and, although she'd never admit it, she was grateful for the warm lump beside her feet as she said goodnight to her husband before flicking the light out and pulling the covers up under her chin.

Chapter 4

MAUREEN SLEPT SURPRISINGLY well and whether it was down to the bicarbonate soda or whether she'd worn herself out with the emotions that had surfaced the night before, she didn't know. Either way, Wednesday, she decided, flinging the covers aside, was going to be a good day. She'd start off by practicing her Sheena Easton in the shower and then she had line dancing at ten o'clock on the dot, in the church hall.

Pooh held a vigil outside the bathroom door, wincing as Maureen hit the high notes.

The first conundrum of the day occurred when Maureen tried to squeeze into the jeans she wore to line dancing. They must have shrunk in the wash given how tight they were around the middle, or was that down to last night's pasta? Pasta always made her bloat, she thought, holding her breath as she zipped them up. She stood in front of the full-length mirror in the spare room and stuck her fingers in the loops of the unforgiving denim before striking a pose. No, it wouldn't do. She couldn't get through a minute of this let alone an hour. It was a yoga pants day, she decided, retrieving the last pair she'd pilfered from Rosi's suitcase when she was over for Aisling's wedding.

'Ah, bliss,' she said out loud once she'd slipped them on—like a second skin they were. There were no belt loops but sure she could stick her thumbs inside the waistband. She did a practise twirl and clap before buttoning up her plaid shirt, knotting it at the bottom, country style! Lastly, she slid her feet into her boots and gave herself a once-over. She still looked the part, she decided, humming *Ruby Don't Take Your Love to Town* as she headed off to make breakfast.

A toast solider was dipped into her soft-boiled egg when the telephone began to shrill. 'That'll be Moira,' she muttered, getting up from the table to answer it, knowing the buttery yolk would be congealed on the toast next time she saw it.

'Good morning, Moira.'

'How did you know it was me?' Jaysus, she was all seeing was Mammy, Moira thought, wondering if she knew in that mysterious mammy way of hers, she was wearing Aisling's black Valentino booties.

'And get your sister's shoes off because there'll be murder if she knows you've been wearing them while she's been away.'

It was spooky, Moira thought, glancing down at the leather booties. It was a shame because they suited the grunge rock chick look, she was after. So what if she was only off to college for the day? She was an adult student at art college where image mattered and as such it was her duty to set the fashion trends for the young ones fresh out of school. She'd risk it, she decided, remembering why she'd rung.

'You were out last night.' Her tone was accusatory.

'I was indeed; is there a problem with my being out, madam?'

'It was Tuesday, Mammy. We always swap notes on *Fair City* on a Tuesday.'

'Not always, Moira. You, yourself, have been out and about on occasion come Tuesday night and did you spare a thought for your poor Mammy at home by herself.'

'You've Pooh to keep you company.' Moira brushed the poor mammy routine aside. 'Where were you? I was worried and so was Roisin.'

'Roisin wouldn't have been worried at all if you hadn't telephoned her.' Maureen pursed her lips.

'Well, I had to because Aisling's over in ABBA land and I was home by myself.'

Maureen sighed. She might as well own up or she'd get no peace. '*I*, was out for dinner with my man-friend, Donal, if you must know.'

'I thought as much.' Moira's eyes narrowed. She had mixed feelings about this Donal business.

'You don't need to sound like I just told you I was prostituting myself on Mabbot Lane.'

'Mammy! Don't be disgusting.'

Maureen was unrepentant. 'We went to a grand Italian place in Raheny, lovely it was too. I had the ravioli and it came with a very nice cream sauce. We had tiramisu for afters, thank you very much for asking.'

'There's no need to be smart, Mammy. I only rang to make sure you were alright. It's my daughterly duty because there're some strange people in this world and you've led a very sheltered life, so. We've not met this Donal fellow. I mean what exactly do we know about him?'

'Moira O'Mara. Don't you be forgetting who's the mammy and who's the child. I am a good judge of character, thanks very much. I married your father, didn't I? Now then, for your information he's not America's Most Wanted he's a widower with two grown-up daughters, one of whom has children of her own. He's gas fitter by trade who's semi-retired and he owns his own home in Drumcondra. He's plenty of money so you don't have to worry he's after mine.' She pushed the image of Patrick aside. He'd make good on his promise, she was sure of it. Should she tell Moira about Donal's hobby? No, she decided, that was a whole other conversation and she'd never get off the phone and back to her soldiers and egg were she to mention she was going to be taking a turn with the microphone, too. 'He's a good man with a kind heart and you'll find that out for yourself soon enough because we're all going to Johnnie Fox's for lunch to get to know one another, his two daughters included once Aisling's back from her honeymoon.'

That gave Moira pause and the wind was momentarily blown from her sails.

'Anyway, I can't be standing around justifying my actions to you all morning, I've a line dancing class to be getting to.'

'Well, I'm busy too you know, but I'm never too busy for my mammy.'

Maureen snorted. She was full of it and she knew as soon as she got off the phone, she'd be burning up the wire ringing Roisin. 'And don't you be ringing Roisin at work either. You'll get her in bother with her boss man, tying her up on personal calls.'

Moira frowned; she really did have the sight she was sure of it.

'Moira, do you hear me? You go and get yourself along to that college of yours and stop worrying yourself about things that are not for you to be worrying about.'

'I hear you.' Moira's nose was out of joint as she hung the phone up, hitting Roisin's work number, which she had on speed dial the moment she heard the dial tone.

Maureen sighed and went back to her breakfast although it was nowhere near as enjoyable as it had been when it was hot. The dishes didn't take long and she ran them through the sink instead of loading the dishwasher. That was another thing about living on your own. It took forever to fill the dishwasher and by the time you had it was beginning to smell and there wasn't so much as a cup left in the place. It was easier to wash-up the old-fashioned way. While the sink filled she looked out the window observing the howling winds of yesterday had settled down, leaving a swept-clean, blue sky in their wake. She wasn't fooled by the calm outlook though, she'd still need her coat. They were a ways off spring yet. *Oh, for the love of God, that cat was back.* She opened the door to the balcony and shooed away Peaches who was sitting on her table eyeballing her in a way that would give you the heebie-jeebies. She'd no ideas of boundaries that cat, she thought, watching its pompom tail slink off around the side of the wall.

Poor Pooh had enough issues as it was, without her sitting there half the day teasing him. She went back inside squeezing past the poodle who'd been observing the goings on. *What to do with him?* It was tempting to take him with her and tie him up outside the entrance to the church hall where he could see what was going on. He loved the line dancing ladies, but again the word 'boundaries' sprang to mind. He'd marked his card with some of them, even though he'd stopped all that sniffing where he shouldn't business since he'd had his little procedure. Rosemary Farrell thought he was the bees knees these days and spoiled him with doggy treats every time she called around. That was going to have to stop if she was going to make headway with the positive reinforcement yoke. 'Will you be a good dog and not howl and carry on while we're trying to do our dancing?'

Pooh panted and gave her a plaintive look.

'Right then, come on I'm giving you the benefit of the doubt, so.'

Maureen was eager to get down there a few minutes early because Rosemary was always early to everything. She was bursting to see her face when she told her she was going to be in a band. She'd be pea green so she would.

Chapter 5

MAUREEN TROTTED ALONG Main Street with Pooh panting at her side making sure she had a firm hold of his leash as they approached Colliers. The butchers, with its window display of tantalising cuts, was his favourite shop in all of Howth. They made it past without incident and he even chose to do his business on the grassy patch beside the public library instead of the pavement which was a first. Sure, we all had to go when we had to go, she thought cheerily, still full of the joys of the night before as she scooped his doings up into one of the bags, she kept in her coat pocket. She popped it in the rubbish bin by the library entrance. She carried more paraphernalia with her for Pooh than she ever had for her babies she mused, giving him a treat before carrying on up the road to where the church loomed.

She could already see several cars parked outside the church and a handful of women milling about on the pavement. She wondered if Rosemary was amongst them. Who'd have thought it? She, Maureen O'Mara, would be singing in a band at her time of life. She was living, breathing proof it was never too late to grab hold of your dream. Actually, her dream had been to play the tambourine on stage, you know like yer Stevie wan from Fleetwood Mac. Perhaps she could do both. Perhaps, she thought, her pace quickening at the idea, she should ring the local paper and tell them. She could be the poster girl for women of a certain age living their best life.

No, she slowed again, she couldn't do that, not when she'd already decided to hold off on letting this latest news slip to Rosi, Aisling or Moira. The lunch would suffice for now. Sure, they didn't need to be privy to all the goings on in her life and the three of them would have a grand old time taking the mick.

'Hello there, Fidelma, Nuala,' she called out as she approached the two women she knew from golf. They were loitering on the pavement beside Nuala's car, looking very ill at ease in their denim jeans and boots. 'First time is it?'

'It is.' Nuala spoke up.

'It's all in the counting; just do what I do and you'll be grand. Have you met Pooh?'

'No.' Both women took a step back, flattening themselves against the zippy blue Honda they'd just exited.

Maureen was unperturbed. 'He won't bite you. He's only after saying hello.'

'It's not biting we're worried about, Maureen,' Nuala muttered. 'Rosemary told us what he was like.'

'Oh no, that's all in the past. He's not bold around the ladies anymore, not since he had the,' she made a scissor motion with her index and middle fingers.

'That might work on your Charlie.' Nuala elbowed Fidelma with a ribald grin.

'Chance would be a fine thing.'

'Are you talking about your dog or your husband?' Maureen asked, not keeping up with the conversation. The sight of Rosemary Farrell limping towards her sidetracked her from the subject of Fidelma's husband. 'I'll see you inside, ladies, and remember, follow my lead in there and you can't go wrong.'

'I don't know how I'll go today, Maureen. My hip's awfully stiff,' Rosemary said, reaching her and bending down to make a fuss of Pooh.

'See,' Maureen called after Nuala and Fidelma. 'He's as saintly as the Pope, these days.' She swivelled back to Rosemary. She found it hard to understand how a hip made of titanium or was it, kryptonite? she could never remember, could get stiff but Rosemary was always after complaining it was paining her. Maybe it was the same as when you lost a limb and had that phantom pain where it used to be. 'Ah well, just do what you can do.'

'What are you wearing?' Rosemary looked up, her eyes fixed on Maureen's trousers.

'My yoga pants. Rosi put me on to them and, Rosemary, I have to say they are the most comfortable trousers I've ever worn. I can do all sorts in them, look,' she lunged forward and back up.

'Well, I wouldn't be able to do that, yoga pants or no yoga pants, not with my hip but they do look comfortable, especially around here.' She patted her middle.

'I don't even know I'm wearing them. Sometimes I have to check I haven't left the house in just my knickers when I've got these on, but listen, before we go in, I've some news to tell you.'

'Oh, yes?' Rosemary was all ears. She was as fond of a bit of harmless gossip as the next woman.

'I had dinner with Donal last night.'

'Maureen O'Mara, if you're going to tell me something that will make me blush—'

'No, not at all, although we did kiss and very nice it was too. It's like riding a bike, Rosemary, once you've got the hang of it you never forget how to do it.'

'I'll take your word for it,' Rosemary said tartly.

'But that's not what I wanted to tell you. He's only after asking me to sing along with him at a birthday bash in Clontarf. He needs me to be Sheena and Dolly.'

'But you can't sing,' Rosemary said, looking as though someone had just squeezed lemon juice on a papercut.

'I can so.' Maureen was affronted although she wasn't surprised, she'd expected a touch of the green eye from Rosemary given she always sang along to the music when they were line dancing, very annoying it was too. She could be an attention seeker could Rosemary. Still and all, maybe she should have a few lessons between now and then to ensure her vocal chords were in top form. There was a woman in town here who gave singing lessons, she'd seen her notice on the wall of the library. Yes, she decided, she'd call in at the library on the way home and get her number.

'Well we can't stand out here all day, best we get inside,' Rosemary said snippily. Maureen followed behind her, pausing to make sure Pooh wasn't going anywhere as she tethered him to the rail outside the entrance. 'Now you behave yourself. Howth's a small town and your reputation precedes you. There's a doggy treat in it for you,' she said, before heading inside the hall.

She took her place up the front of the class, smiling and greeting the twenty or so group of women. Word was spreading, she thought. There'd only been fifteen of them a few weeks back. It wasn't just good from a physical exercise perspective either. Laura, their instructor, who was in her thirties and had young children at home, had told them line dancing was good for memory and exercising the brain as well. She was very good was Laura. Maureen liked the fact she always wore a white Stetson to match her white boots and she was young enough to get away with a short skirt unlike Joan Fairbrother down the back there. It was important to look the part, Maureen believed, if you wanted to be taken seriously.

Laura had spent time in America in cowboy country as she called it and had fallen in love with line dancing while she was there. Maureen would have liked to have asked her why she hadn't fallen in love with a cowboy while she was over there. You know, like the ones you saw on the covers of those romance books. The fellas who fill out their open necked shirts and jeans in a way not many Irish sheep or beef farmers ever would. Instead she'd come home and married Ned Perkins, a local real estate agent, who looked like he'd topple over in a gusty breeze.

Laura was intent on getting them to master her three favourite dances, the Tush Push, the Slap Leather and the Boot Scootin Boogie. Maureen could see why Rosemary struggled with the Tush Push. Personally speaking, her favourite was the Boot Scootin Boogie.

Laura clapped her hands but the chatter carried on and Maureen turned around and put a finger to her lips to shush everyone. Good manners were next to godliness. They finally quietened down and Laura introduced herself and gave the new attendees a run-down on who she was and what her credentials were to teach this style of dance as well as touting its health benefits. Then, she clapped her hands and said they were good to go before pushing play on her portable stereo. Today, they were starting off with the Tush Push. Maureen side-eyed Rosemary, she wouldn't be happy with all the gyrating they were in for. Served her right, she thought, concentrating on her heel, toe, heel. She liked the music, Laura had chosen. It was that Shania one, singing about wanting to feel a man.

The class was over quickly and Maureen thought the high-fiving that Nuala and Fidelma did at the end was a little over the top. As for Pooh, he'd been remarkably well behaved throughout the hour-long class and she wondered if it was the country music. It seemed to have a soothing effect on him. 'Thank you, Laura,' she called to the young woman who was packing her things away.

'Great job today, Maureen, you were on fire.'

'Thanks very much.' Ha, take that, Rosemary, she thought, still annoyed by her earlier comment.

She felt a tap on the shoulder as she was heading out the door. It was Nuala. 'Maureen, I was admiring your moves in there. You're a natural, so you are. Those trousers you're after wearing look grand on you, too especially around here.' She slapped her own bottom. Yes, Maureen thought, Nuala was getting very caught up in the American side of line dancing. Still and all, a compliment was a compliment and she was nothing if not gracious.

'Thank you, Nuala. It's the shape of them you see, they can turn a pear into a peach. My Rosi put me on to them.' She pulled the fabric away. 'Feel how soft they are.'

Nuala rubbed the fabric between her thumb and forefinger. 'Lovely and soft. Fidelma, feel this.'

Fidelma did so. 'They are,' she agreed before adding, 'I'm not getting on with these jeans.' Nuala nodded her agreement.

'Me neither. They ride up where they've no business going riding. Those trousers you're wearing would do me nicely.'

'Ah well, I'm sorry, ladies, I can't help you there. Rosi buys them in London.'

Nuala pursed her lips in disappointment.

'Can you not ask her to get us a pair each?' Fidelma asked.

Maureen felt the stirrings of an idea. She untied Pooh who was definitely going to be getting a treat in a moment and said. 'Listen, ladies, leave it with me would you, and I'll see what I can do.'

'You could put me down for a pair too,' Rosemary said. 'There's no flexibility in these.' She gestured to her dark denim jeans.

'What's that you're all on about?' Marian asked, joining them out the front, Mary and Agnes peering over her shoulder to see what all the fuss was about.

By the time Maureen set off for home she had ten orders for yoga pants and a business plan was beginning to form. She walked briskly, keen to telephone Rosi.

Chapter 6

MAUREEN CONVENIENTLY forgot about her having told Moira just that morning not to be ringing Roisin when she was at work. She peered at the number scrawled in her telephone book and tapped it out waiting impatiently for her eldest daughter to answer. She wouldn't normally ring London at this time of the day, what with it being peak rates, but this was important and besides, if things went to plan, she'd be able to claim the call as a business expense. Roisin's dulcet tones reverberated down the line.

'Rosi, it's your mammy.'

'Is everything alright, Mammy, you don't normally ring me at work.'

'Everything is grand. Now, I want you to listen carefully as to what I'm about to say.'

'Mammy, you're not a spy in the cold war.'

'Don't be clever, Roisin, this is important. I'm after having a brainwave.'

'Did it hurt?'

Maureen ignored her. 'I want to host a Tupperware party except instead of Tupperware we'd be selling yoga pants. What do you think?'

'I think you're mad.'

'No, hear me out, Roisin. You told me you buy the yoga pants off a local market. Well, what you do is buy up big and bring them over here with you and we put a decent mark-up on them. I'll have nibbles and drinks organised here to get the ladies in the mood for spending and when they're nicely relaxed you can do a demonstration of your bendy yoga. They'll be so impressed by the way you can lunge and touch your toes and things they'll have to splash the cash. We split the profit and we're laughing all the way to the bank.'

Over in London, Roisin was holding the phone away from her ear, looking at it with a frown on her face as she shook her head. Her family were mad the lot of them. She'd already had Moira on the phone last night worrying over where Mammy was and again this morning going on about her having been on a dinner date with her man-friend. She'd prattled on about how Mammy had mentioned a luncheon where they were going to meet him officially. Roisin was looking forward to Aisling returning from her honeymoon so Mammy and Moira had someone else to annoy.

'Come on, Rosi, I need you on board. I can't do it without you bringing the gear in. I'll take care of your airfares.'

Oh, for fecks sake, now Mammy sounded like she was organising for her to smuggle drugs in on Ryan Air. Then again, a free trip to Dublin to see Shay was not to be sniffed at. 'What about sizes and things how would you know how many of each to order?' She'd not thought this madcap idea of hers through properly.

Maureen visualised the line dancing ladies, the golfing ladies, the yacht club ladies, the water colour painting class ladies and the bowls ladies. 'Large, and one or two mediums would do the trick.'

'I'll think about it.'

Rosi hadn't been nicknamed easy-osi Rosi by her family for nothing and she knew her mammy well enough to know she had the bit firmly between her teeth on this one and wouldn't let it go until she got her way. 'Alright, alright. I'll do it.'

Chapter 7

BRONAGH FINISHED TAPPING the reservation, that had come through the fax machine two minutes ago from a German tour operator, into the computer. She was using far more force on the keyboard than was necessary, not that taking her current mood out on it was making her feel any better. She carefully noted down the reservation in the book she kept beside the Mac as backup because she refused to put all her faith in the computer, before opening her drawer. She retrieved the custard creams snaffling one down and then another. What did it matter if she put the weight back on she'd worked so hard to lose for Aisling's wedding? Who cared? She could pinpoint the moment when she'd begun to feel out of sorts; not grumpy as such, well, a little yes but it was mingled with a malaise that was most unlike her.

This current frame of mind had descended when Moira had breezed through reception in a pair of boots Bronagh was certain didn't belong to her. When she'd pointed this out, Moira had ignored the part about the boots not belonging to her and informed Bronagh this particular style was called a bootie, not a boot per se. She thought she was awfully clever now she was at the college, Bronagh had thought. Moira had attempted to con a custard cream from her as was her usual morning routine. Now, Bronagh was glad she'd only let her have one of the biscuits because she needed them more than Moira did.

Moira had put the whole thing in her mouth and perched on the edge of the desk, brushing the crumbs from her jeans before telling her what was on her mind. 'I spoke to Mammy this morning.'

'Oh yes? And how is your mammy, I haven't seen her for the best part of a week?'

'Well that's because she's busy with her new man-friend.' Moira registered the look of surprise on Bronagh's face with satisfaction. It was validation Mammy was indeed being secretive. 'She's not mentioned him to you either, then? I'm not surprised, she's been very cagey about the whole thing. Although, she mentioned organising a lunch so Rosi, Aisling and myself can meet him and his daughters, which I'm taking to mean she's serious about him. It makes me feel weird, Bronagh, to think of Mammy with anyone other than Daddy.' Moira shuddered.

Bronagh had been sharper than she'd normally be with the youngest of the O'Mara girls but her tongue had taken on a life of its own. 'Now listen to me, Moira O'Mara. You're not to be raining on your mammy's parade. Sure, you and your sisters are grown women with lives of your own and she's entitled to some happiness. It doesn't mean she loved your daddy any less if she steps out with someone new.'

Moira had been a little taken aback. She'd expected custard creams and a sympathetic ear not getting the head eaten off her. She'd tottered out the door in the heeled booties with a wounded air.

Bronagh had been banging about ever since and not even the half packet of custard creams she was chomping her way through was helping matters. She was happy Maureen had someone she was sweet on. It had been her shoulder that had been leaned on by her old employer and good friend after Brian's death. It had nearly crushed her but she'd gritted her teeth and gotten on with things because that's what you did. She was still a woman in the prime of her life so, why shouldn't she have a second chance at happiness? She didn't begrudge her it at all but what had her upset was knowing she'd never even gotten her first chance at happiness and Moira's words this morning had brought back all those old feelings of resentment that did her no good whatsoever. Normally she kept a tight lid on them but they'd pushed their way out and she couldn't seem to shove them back in their box. There was nobody to blame for the way things had worked out other than herself. She'd made her choices and sure she had a good life. It was only it had felt back then as if she'd had no choice. None at all.

Chapter 8

1970

'HERE WE GO, MAM.' BRONAGH put a cup of tea down on the tray table beside her mother. Myrna Hanrahan was sitting in the mustard coloured armchair with its white crocheted antimacassars protecting the fabric beneath its fat velveteen arms. Her sparrow-like frame was dwarfed by the plump cushions and she had a woollen patchwork blanket thrown across her knees. She was dressed and her dark hair which had more than a dash of silver running through it was curling prettily around her cheeks, the way it did when it had been freshly washed. These were good signs insomuch that she must have gone out despite being so poorly, hopefully to see their family doctor. Her green blouse was buttoned right to the top the bow done up and Bronagh could see the hem of her skirt in a paler shade of green peeking out from beneath the blanket. She had tights on and her feet were in her sheepskin-lined slippers, even though the sun was shining outside.

The chair had been Dad's favourite when he was alive. Sometimes Bronagh imagined she could see him sitting there with his paper held open, puffing on his pipe. It was a glimpse of happier memories that were beginning to fade. If she leaned in close though, she could still catch a whiff of his Condor ready rubbed tobacco. The scent of old barber shops and burnt toast that had curled from his pipe was that of her dad. Her mam had commandeered his chair of late because it was the

46

softest one in the house. She said it didn't hurt her bones like the others with their springy cushions. Bronagh struggled to understand what she meant by her bones hurting but the fact her mam's face was pale and drawn with lines of pain etched around her eyes was plain for anyone to see.

Hilary, Bronagh's elder and only sibling had made her promise she'd go and see Doctor Burke today. It was high time she got to the bottom of why she'd been having these spells where her body ached all over and she didn't have the energy to get out of bed. It had all begun with a nasty chill she'd picked up which she'd not been able to shake and Bronagh had chewed her fingernails down worrying about the dizziness her mam was suffering along with all her other symptoms. She was terrified she'd collapse and bang her head while she was at work. It wasn't like any chill Bronagh had ever had.

Bronagh had to enlist Hilary's help in convincing Mam to go the doctor that first time too, no easy task given Myrna was a woman who didn't believe in bothering important people like Doctor Burke over the likes of aches and pains. She needed to rest that was all, she'd croak each time Bronagh broached the topic of her going, but she'd listened to Hilary. As it happened Doctor Burke had said more or less the same thing. Her illness was viral so there was no need for antibiotics and with an 'I told you so' Myrna had taken to her bed.

She'd seemed to get better to Bronagh's relief but then a month later she'd gone to the shops and returned home completely exhausted. The butchers and corner shop were only at the end of the road. No more than a ten minute walk each way including stopping to chat to the neighbours out and about doing the same thing. It was more than the virus she'd had leaving her feeling washed out because she'd not been out of bed for the five days following. This was so unlike her mam, who prided herself on keeping busy and running a tight ship at home, Bronagh had taken it upon herself to telephone Hilary once more.

She'd regretted making the call the moment she'd heard her sister's haughty hello down the line. She'd pictured her standing in the hallway of her big house in Tramore. She'd be beside the telephone table where she always had a vase of fresh flowers, twirling the cord of the telephone in that way of hers.

Hilary was a very self-important housewife who'd married a solicitor. Her husband George had been working for a Dublin firm when she met him. He was staid with his dull suits and short back and sides when all the other fellas were beginning to wear their hair a touch too long, but he had good prospects. Good prospects mattered to Hilary who'd always imagined herself somewhere fancier than the two bedroomed terrace where she'd grown up, where Bronagh still lived with her mam. She and George had married and moved to his hometown of Tramore by the seaside in County Waterford not long after and he'd opened a practice there. Hilary was a lady of leisure these days, or at least she was between the hours of eight thirty and three o'clock now her two children, Declan and Erin, were both at school. She had a cleaning woman who came once a week and a man who did the garden. What her sister did with herself all day was a mystery to Bronagh.

There'd never been much love lost between the pair of them who were as different as night and day. Myrna would shake her head and wonder how two girls who were made by the same Mammy and Daddy could be so different. Bronagh hadn't a clue; it was just the way it was and a fat lot of good Hilary had been when she'd said she was worried about their mam, too. The conversation had played out as she'd expected and she'd been annoyed at herself for hoping this time might be different.

'Doctor Burke said it was viral last time she went and it's probably still in her system. These things can hang about for a long while you know,' Hilary had said, as though she were an expert on the subject of mystery viruses. 'I don't know what you expect me to do about it from here, Bronagh? I'm not exactly around the corner, now am I? And I can't drop everything because Mam's a little under the weather.' She'd been defensive. 'I've a family to be thinking of.'

And don't we know it, Bronagh had thought. It was her sister's trump card. 'I, didn't ask you to drop everything.' She hadn't rung to fight and bit back the question as to what she'd be dropping exactly. Her bridge club or luncheon with The Wives of the Businessmen of Tramore Society perhaps? She'd made that up but it was the sort of thing Hilary would swan along to, were it to exist. She'd tried to keep her voice steady because this wasn't about her and Hilary, it was about Mam. 'I'm trying to explain to you it's more than her being under the weather, I'm sure of it. She was better, back to her old self and then after she took herself down to the shops, she just crashed. Her memory's not right either, Hilary. She's forgetting things which isn't like her. Mam's sharp as a tack usually. I'm worried and I thought you'd want to be kept in the loop.'

'I do.'

'Well then, I was hoping you'd talk some sense into her and get her to go back to Doctor Burke again. She pooh-poohs the idea whenever I bring it up but she listens to you. I'd take her myself but I've only just started at O'Mara's. Do you remember the Georgian guesthouse by St Stephen's Green?

'Yes, I remember it.'

Not so much as a hint of interest in her voice, Bronagh thought, not knowing why this stung even though she'd expected no different. 'Well, I'm their new receptionist and I don't want to be asking for time off so soon in the picture.' She'd had a bright idea. 'Could Mam come and stay with you for a week or so? The salt air might perk her up and she hasn't seen the children in a good while.'

She'd heard the horror in Hilary's voice, aghast at the very idea. 'So, you'd have Declan and Erin catching whatever it is Mam's picked up, would you?'

'I don't think it's contagious, Hilary. I never got it. Sure, I'm fit as a fiddle.'

There'd been a weighty sigh. 'Well I can't risk it. What sort of a mother would that make me? Go and fetch her. I'll have a word.'

'I'll see if I can get her to come downstairs. She's in bed.'

'At this time of the day?'

Bronagh had rolled her eyes. Had her sister not listened to a word she'd been saying?

'I haven't got all day. The children will be wanting their tea soon.'

Bronagh's hand had trembled with rage as she put the receiver down on the shelf where the telephone sat and she'd taken a steadying breath before calling, 'Mammy,' as she took to the stairs. She'd poked her head around the bedroom door dismayed to find the room dark despite it being light still outside.

It was stuffy and smelt of skin and the washing liquid they used for their laundry. She'd open the curtains and the windows a crack to let some fresh air in, in a minute. 'Mammy, Hilary's on the telephone wanting a word.' She'd moved closer to the bed and two eyes had blinked up at her. Her mam's dressing gown was sprawled at the bottom of the bed and she'd picked it up. 'C'mon now. She's waiting. Can you sit up?'

'Hilary's on the phone?' There'd been a spark in her mam's weary voice at the mention of her eldest daughter. 'Help me up, Bronagh. There's a girl. It's good of her to call. She's very busy you know, what with the children and running that house of hers.'

Bronagh had wanted to snort. It irked her the way her mam put her selfish mare of a sister on a pedestal when she was the one who worked full time, but making a snidey remark wouldn't help matters. 'Here we are pop this on, Mam.' She'd held out her dressing gown for her and when she'd slipped her arms inside it, she'd belted it closed. She'd kept a tight hold of her arm as she helped her down the stairs. How they'd manage the coming back up, she didn't know. She'd cross that bridge when she came to it. Her mam's body seemed to be giving up on her and, not trusting her ability to stand on her own for long, she'd dragged a chair in from the kitchen for her to sit on. She'd waited beside her until she'd sat down and said, 'Hello.' before taking herself off into the kitchen to put the potatoes on to boil. She who'd nothing important to do with her time if Hilary were to be believed! She'd kept her ear cocked to see how the conversation played out.

'The doctor's, you say?' Her mam's voice had sounded thin, reedy almost. There was silence as she'd listened to whatever it was Hilary was saying. 'Ah now, you know Bronagh can be dramatic. I'm a little tired that's all, but yes, if it makes you feel better, I promise I'll go tomorrow. How are the children? Are they about?'

Her grandchildren's voices would have been a tonic for her mam, Bronagh had thought, but Hilary had already ended the call.

'She's very busy. She's a function to go to this evening and she had to give the children their tea.' Myrna had excused her eldest daughter's rush to get off the phone as she appeared in the kitchen doorway, Bronagh turned the boiling water down a notch and pulled out a chair for her.

'Sit down, Mam,' she'd said, before tossing the sausages in the fry pan. She'd heard her mam sigh over the top of the hissing, spitting sausages.

'I don't know why you're always prickly when it comes to your sister.'

'I'm not.'

'You are, I can see it in the set of your shoulders now. You shouldn't be worrying her like that either. She's enough on her plate. I'm alright, you know, but if it means you'll stop panicking and telling all and sundry your old mam's on death's door, I'll go and see Doctor Burke tomorrow.'

Bronagh had stabbed a fat sausage with a fork, that was something at least.

Now, as her mam sipped her tea, she asked her how she'd gotten on. 'What did Doctor Burke have to say this time around Mam, has he given you anything to take?'

'He couldn't find anything wrong with me. I'm worn out that's all. He thought it might be women's problems. This here,' she raised her teacup, 'is better than any pills he could prescribe.'

Bronagh shook her head and left her to enjoy her tea. It was like banging her head against a brick wall trying to get anywhere. Women's problems, was a broad term for I haven't a clue what's wrong with you, she thought, taking herself off to the kitchen to peel the potatoes and carrots to go in the hotpot she was making for their dinner.

Present

The fax clicking and whirring into life brought Bronagh back to the here and now. She'd never thought she'd become a caregiver. It was a role that had sneaked up on her. It wasn't as though she'd gone for an interview as she'd done for this job, here at O'Mara's. There'd been no reference from her previous employer to hand over to be glanced at. She hadn't had to smile and put her best foot forward, it had simply happened. A gradual slide as her mam's bouts of being unwell had continued to recur. She'd thought, as most women her age back then had done, she'd marry and have children, taken it for granted she'd do so in fact. Kevin had wanted to marry her, she was sure of it, even if he hadn't gotten around to asking her. It wasn't meant to be, though. She wouldn't think about him. It would do nothing to improve her mood. Bronagh didn't believe in regrets but if she did, she'd regret the way things had turned out. Her sigh came from deep within her as she got up from the seat to see what the machine behind her was spitting out.

Chapter 9

MAUREEN BUSTLED INTO her old stamping ground, the guesthouse, where things were ticking over nicely in Aisling's absence. She'd left Pooh at home this morning having loaded her stereo with country music CDs and setting it to random selection. He'd given a mournful howl as she'd pushed play and edged her way out the door, which Maureen was certain was an attempt at singing along with Loretta Lynn. He really was very clever, she thought, sneaking out the door and leaving him to it.

She hadn't come to O'Mara's to check up on the staff; they were all perfectly capable of managing on their own for the fortnight, Aisling was away. All of them, except perhaps, Ita. Maureen might give her a gentle rally today and it wouldn't do any harm to check on the rooms that were expecting guests tonight to ensure they were up to standard. She was young, Ita, and needed to be steered in the right direction until she could find her place in the world. Maureen had a soft spot for their director of housekeeping as she called herself because she knew she'd had a tough time when her dad had left, as had her mammy, Maureen's old friend. As for Bronagh, whose dark head she could make out behind the enormous vase of blooms, she'd worked for them for thirty odd years and could run the place with her eyes shut, and her hands tied behind her back too, come to that. She was more than their receptionist, she was part of the furniture, she was family.

'How're ye, Bronagh,' she trilled. She had the paper she wanted her to type and print off the computer clutched in her hand. In her other was a brown paper bag in which she had two fresh, sugar topped ginger-snap cookies. They were so fresh they were still warm and she knew Bronagh was partial to anything ginger—anything sweet, more to the point. She was easy to please was Bronagh.

Bronagh jumped, she'd been so engrossed in the letter she was reading she hadn't heard the door open. She swiftly tucked the piece of paper away in her top drawer beside the replenished biscuit stock. Its arrival along with this morning's post, which in Aisling's absence she was taking care of, had done wonders to lift the fug that had settled over her these past few days. The letters had been arriving like clockwork once a week since Christmas; she wrote back with equal regularity. It had all begun with a Christmas card addressed to her personally which had been sent here to the guesthouse. These letters warmed her and lifted her spirits during the bleak wintery weeks. She hoped hers were having the same effect across the water there.

'Grand, Maureen. Yourself?'

'Oh, I can't complain.'

'No, I hear not.'

Maureen appeared around the side of the desk with narrowed eyes. 'Moira?'

'Moira,' Bronagh confirmed.

'Jaysus wept, that girl! Shall I make us a cup of tea so we can enjoy our morning treat?' She held up the paper bag.

'A grand plan, Maureen,' Bronagh said as the gently spiced aroma of ginger teased her.

The guests' lounge was deserted and Maureen set about making the tea and running an eye over the place. She'd tell Ita it could do with a dust. Bronagh was on the telephone when she came back in and placed the cups and saucers carefully down on the front desk. She disappeared again and returned a moment later with two side plates for their biscuits. The door burst open before she could take so much as a bite or sip and, with Bronagh still on the phone, Maureen snapped back into her old role.

'Good morning and welcome to O'Mara's.' Her eyes widened at the sight of the tall, thin man, clad in tweed with a matching cap on top of his head. He had a clipboard in his hand and looked like he'd just got off the bus from the Village of Back of Beyond. His smile, revealing a missing tooth, cemented her first impression. The more she stared the more she thought he had a look of Colm, one of her Brother's Grimm about him.

'Ruaraidh's the name,' it came out as a lisped, 'Rory.'

'And a grand name it is too. What can I be doing for you today?' All that was missing was a piece of straw between his teeth.

'I'm here to pick up a couple from America.' He looked at the clipboard he held in his hand. 'The Claremonts from Virginia. I'm their tour guide.'

Sweet and Merciful Jesus! What impression would the couple take home of Ireland with him as their guide? Maureen thought, with a shake of her head.

Bronagh put the phone down and finished scribbling the message she'd taken before peering over at Ruaraidh. 'I'll ring their room and tell them you're here.'

'Where's the pretty red-headed girl?' Ruaraidh leered about the place.

Yes, he definitely reminded Maureen of her brother, Colm. 'On her honeymoon,' she said in a clipped voice, to quell any ideas he might be having under that tweed cap of his. A huffing and puffing akin to a train pulling into its stop sounded behind her and she spun around to see their breakfast cook, Mrs Flaherty. She was even redder in the cheeks than normal, if possible.

'Maureen, I thought I heard your voice.'

Holy God Above Tonight! The woman had better hearing than a bat, Maureen thought, taking a step back as Mrs Flaherty drew breath before launching into her speech.

'It's no fecking good. Something's got to be done about that fecking fox!'

Ruiraidh's eyes popped at the apparition in the apron as he thought to himself, surely she was a woman who should be baking apple pie not cursing like a sailor?

At least it had stopped him poking his head about the place to see if Maureen was only teasing when she'd said Aisling was away because she was in fact hiding behind the sofa. It was either that or he was checking for dust.

The Claremonts appeared on the landing, each clutching a suitcase. Poor Mrs Claremont was holding the cross around her neck as if to ward off the spectre of the swearing Irish cook.

Maureen went into damage control. 'Mrs Flaherty, come back downstairs with me and we'll see if we can't sort this out. Good morning to you, Mr and Mrs Claremont. You're in for a grand day to start your tour of our fair isle today so you are, there's definitely a hint of blue under those rain clouds. Mark my words, the sun will be shining in an hour.'

The forecast was for rain and more rain followed by rain but they didn't need to know that, she thought, beaming up at them before herding Mrs Flaherty back to the kitchen. Bronagh better not eat her ginger snap as well as her own, was her last thought before she began to pacify the cook who was threatening to storm the Iveagh Gardens behind them where the little red fox was holed up, her rolling pin her weapon. Foxy Loxy had paid a visit the night before by all accounts and left a telltale trail of debris all the way to his hole under the bricked wall.

By the time she'd returned, having made promises of sealing holes up she had no intention of keeping, reception was quiet once more and her tea was stone cold. Bronagh who had indeed been eyeing her ginger snap had thought better of helping herself and instead had gotten up to waft the air freshener about.

'That Ruiraidh fellow smelled of horses,' she said. 'I wouldn't fancy being shut in a bus with him for hours on end.'

Maureen breathed in the Arpège fragranced freshener she'd bought for the guesthouse, pleased it was being used.

'It reminds me of you, this does, Maureen. Whenever Aisling's after spraying it about the place I'm always looking over my shoulder expecting to see you there.' She put the cap back on the canister and sat down. Maureen perched on the edge of the fax table and both women settled in for a good chat.

'So, what's his name and what's he like this fella of yours, and is he a toy boy?' Bronagh watched as Maureen's face seemed to come alive as she described him.

'He's five years older than me. His name's Donal, Donal McCarthy and he's a widower.' She gave Bronagh the same spiel she'd given Moira, adding. 'And he's kind and generous. He makes me laugh and when I'm around him I feel young again.'

Bronagh felt wistful stirrings. 'Is he a silver fox then?'

'No, I'd say more a silver bear.' She polished off her ginger biscuit deciding she could trust Bronagh and besides, she wanted to confide in someone who would be excited for her not like the old bionic hip of Howth, Rosemary Farrell. 'He's a dead ringer for Kenny Rogers and he sings in a Kenny Rogers Tribute band.'

'I love *Coward of the County*.' Bronagh was animated as she hummed the old tune. 'Does he wear the white suit with the waistcoat. A natty dresser is Kenny.'

'He does and Donal does a very good rendition of *Coward of the County*. Although, I prefer *The Gambler* myself. Bronagh, don't be breathing a word about his hobby to Moira, will you? She's been making enough wisecracks as it is. I'd rather she met him without any preconceptions.'

'Fair play to you, but these things have a way of getting out, Maureen. It won't be thanks to me though and I'm happy for you,' Bronagh said, and she meant it.

Maureen leaned over and patted the receptionist's hand. 'You're the first person to say that to me. Thank you, Bronagh, it means a lot to me.'

'Are the girls taking a bit of getting used to the idea then or is it just one in particular?'

'Moira?'

Bronagh nodded.

'She was very close to her daddy being the baby of the family and all.'

'Ah, don't be making excuses for her. They all were, Maureen, and as I said to Moira the other day, just because your mammy's met someone who's making her happy doesn't mean she's stopped loving your daddy. It doesn't diminish what they had.'

Maureen's eyes burned with threatened tears and she sniffed in an effort to keep them at bay, blinking rapidly. 'Oh, Bronagh, I'm frightened they're all going to hate each other on sight.'

'Who?'

'His daughters, Louise and Anna, and my three. Donal's wanting to organise a lunch for us all to meet when Aisling's back and Roisin's next over. He says he feels like we're sneaking around the place and he's too long in the tooth for that.'

'That sounds a very sensible thing to do and I think you're worrying over nothing. Once the girls have seen for themselves, Donal's a nice man with good intentions toward their mammy, they'll be grand. It's the unknown you see. They've vivid imaginations your three, they'll be picturing all sorts.'

Maureen thought about yer busking one who whistled through the gap where his front teeth used to be.

'What does Patrick have to say?'

'I haven't spoken to Patrick since he went to America. That's another thing, Bronagh. I did something that's weighing heavily on me.'

Bronagh waited, not wanting to interrupt Maureen's flow.

'I loaned him some money.'

'A lot of money?'

Maureen nodded. 'He wanted it for a venture he said was a sure thing. He's promised to pay it back before the year's out. It's just—'

'It's not sitting well with you.'

'No, it's not. I feel as though I've the indigestion whenever I think about it.'

'You haven't told the girls?'

'No, they'd be on the telephone giving out to him.'

Bronagh shook her head. She was fond of Patrick, having known him since he was a young boy but he had a streak in him that one. He was out for himself and it wasn't right putting the squeeze on his mammy for cash. 'He's your son, Maureen. You'll have to trust him.'

Maureen pursed her lips. 'I do trust him, it's just he's not very reliable. You're a good woman, Bronagh, so you are, listening to my moans.' She almost wished she'd let Bronagh have her other biscuit now. It would have been the good Christian thing to do. 'And how's your mam doing?'

'She's having a good spell at the moment, been scrapbooking like a demon so she has. She's off down to Tramore in two weeks and counting down the days. I'll tell her you were asking after her.'

'Be sure to. It's a terrible thing that ME and her struck down with it so young.'

'It is and there's those a lot younger than she was suffering with it. I've seen a young woman barely out of college at the support meetings she goes to from time to time.' It had taken years of, 'It's in her head' for a diagnosis as to what ailed her mam to finally be given and when it had come it had still been vague and inconclusive because the doctors knew so little about the disease but at least Myrna had felt validated.

'Does your neighbour still look in on her during the day when you're here?'

'Sara? Yes, she's very good to her. She pops over most days and makes her a cup of tea and stays for a chat. The health nurse calls in twice a week too.' It meant Bronagh didn't have to worry about her being on her own all day while she was working. 'She goes to her club of a Friday, too.'

A clattering down the stairs made them both pause and turn in time to see a young man with a briefcase in his hand. He gave them a cursory wave as he whirled through reception and out the door.

'Mr Cleary from Room 4. Late for a meeting's my guess,' Bronagh said.

'Hm, must have overslept,' Maureen said. She remembered what it was that had brought her to O'Mara's today. 'I came here to ask a favour of you. Would you mind typing this for me?'

Bronagh took the handwritten sheet from her and said out loud, 'You're invited to a Yoga Pants Party. What's this all about then?'

'You've heard of Tupperware parties?'

'Of, course I have.' Bronagh could recall having gone to more than one back in the early seventies and spending a small fortune on storage containers. Mind they'd been handy in their day. 'Hasn't everybody got a Tupperware container with no fecking lid lurking down the back of their cupboard?'

'True enough.' Maureen had a brown canister that had cost her a pretty penny when the children were small. She'd been convinced by yer woman hosting the do, her life wouldn't be the same without this superior piece of kitchenware keeping her spaghetti noodles fresh. It had long since lost its lid somewhere or other. 'But it's nothing to do with Tupperware.'

'I know that. It says yoga pants party but you brought up the Tupperware.'

They were getting sidetracked and Maureen was glad she wasn't in a rush because it looked like she was going to have to start at the beginning. 'What it is, Bronagh, is this. I was at my line dancing class this week and I wore my yoga pants instead of my jeans on account of the jeans cutting off my circulation around my middle.'

Bronagh made a noise indicating she knew where Maureen was coming from.

'They were so comfortable, like wearing no pants at all and I still looked the part doing the Tush Push. Afterward, all the ladies were asking where they could get a pair for themselves and that's when I had the idea for the party. Rosi's on board, she's going to be my supplier. You can have yours at cost if you come along to the church hall, your mammy's more than welcome too. We'll have drinks and nibbles. It'll be grand. And I'm going to get Rosi to do a demonstration of all her bendy yoga moves so everyone can see what you can get up to in the yoga pants.' Aisling would be back by then and if she'd been holiday-eating she'd probably be wanting a pair of yoga pants to be getting about in herself. Moira could come and help her and Rosi set it up, as penance for being a cheeky mare this last while.

Bronagh began tip-tapping the invitation out. She liked the sound of these yoga pants.

Chapter 10

MAUREEN SET OFF FOR home having had a quiet word in Ita's ear about what needed doing about the guesthouse, leaving their young director of housekeeping with the impression she'd be calling back later on without actually saying so. She'd left her hurrying off to the cleaning supplies cupboard and, satisfied all was as it should be at O'Mara's, Maureen set off with the neatly typed invitation in her hand. She'd plans to call in at Reads to get copies run off and would multi-task once back in Howth by distributing them to her various groups as well as taking Pooh for a walk.

Meanwhile, Bronagh, sitting behind her desk, eyed the date of the party, the invitation still on her screen. It was on a Thursday evening in just on two weeks. She was looking forward to it and not because her skirt was once more straining at the middle because she couldn't very well wear yoga pants to work, now could she? Mind, Maureen had said they could be dressed up or down. What she was looking forward to most with regard to the party was sharing it with Leonard. She looked forward to sharing all the ins and outs of her day-to-day goings on with him. She opened her desk drawer, bypassed the biscuits and retrieved the latest letter she'd been poring over when Maureen had called in.

Most of the guests were out and about and the pile of reservations waiting to be entered into the computer could wait until she'd read through it again properly. She wanted the opportunity to savour the letter for a while. Leonard, or Mr Walsh as she'd always thought of him until his unexpected Christmas card, would be back in Dublin come September and although Bronagh knew how time had a way of running away on itself, September seemed a long ways off. He came every year at the same time, staying at O'Mara's in the same room, and had done so for years. He'd leave his home in Liverpool to visit his sister who still lived in the house he'd grown up in here in the city. He maintained his reason for not staying in his old family home was so as to put some distance between himself and his sister, a necessity if he wanted to keep his sanity during his visits.

The tone of the letters was conversational and, as she read them, Bronagh imagined she was having a cosy chat with a good friend. A little like she'd just done with Maureen only it was different because she'd get a fluttering sense of anticipation as she began to read them. The letters from Leonard were her secret, and a delicious one at that.

'Who's that you're writing to, Bronagh?' Myrna had asked seeing Bronagh putting pen to paper for the first time in a very long while, the television humming in the background.

'I've a pen pal, Mam, in Liverpool.'

'Liverpool!' Myrna snorted. 'Couldn't you have found somewhere more exotic than Liverpool? Sure, the world's a big place you know, Bronagh.'

Bronagh carried on writing. 'There's nothing wrong with Liverpool, Mam, it was home to the Beatles after all and besides, my pen pal's very well-travelled.' He was too. He'd been a shipwright in the navy and had seen the world. Each week he shared an anecdote from this time and she looked forward to reading it because she was seeing a little of the world through his eyes.

'I'm not saying there is and I'm as fond of Paul McCartney as any other red-blooded woman but I'm saying you could have struck up a friendship with someone from Australia or New Zealand for instance. I'd have liked to have heard what it's like to live on the other side of the world with kangaroos and snakes and things. How did you come to be writing to this lass in Liverpool anyway?'

Bronagh hadn't corrected her mother's assumption her pen pal was a woman nor did she tell her there weren't any kangaroos or snakes in New Zealand, not that she'd ever heard of at any rate. Instead she was economical with the truth. 'A guest, Mam, who stayed at O'Mara's, we struck up a friendship and decided to keep in touch.'

'Well, I suppose they had yer Cilla Black one too, she'd a lovely voice,' Myrna had said, wincing as she shifted in the armchair trying to get comfortable.

Now, Bronagh glared at the telephone daring it to ring while she took five minutes to scan the familiar old-school handwriting.

Dear Bronagh,

The sun's been shining this week and I saw my first daffodil while I was walking Bessie. The warmer weather's doing wonders for her old bones, and mine! It's far too early for spring bulbs of course but it brought a smile to my face as did the rise in temperature. Winter seems to go on for such a long time, don't you think? While summer passes in the blink of an eye. Last Sunday I went to see an afternoon session of Erin Brockovich. You know the film people are talking about. Very good it was too. I think you'd enjoy it although you might think twice about drinking water straight from your, kitchen tap again. Julia Roberts played her part well too. Normally I find it hard to take her seriously with that enormous mouth of hers but she did herself proud. Hats off to Julia.

Some good news, Harry and I ended our month-long losing streak by winning at bowls this week and we enjoyed a celebratory pub lunch and pint or two after. The Duke of York does a lovely roast. I can't remember the last time I had roast pork with crackling and apple sauce not to mention the plumpest Yorkshire puddings you've ever seen. It went down a treat.

This week I thought I'd tell you about the time the Orwell docked in Montevideo, Uruguay. I'd not long turned twenty-one and didn't know much about much and all I knew about Uruguay was, it's home to the gaucho. This conjured up wide open spaces and sprawling estancias. The other fact I was aware of was the people love football and eat lots of meat. So, it was a pleasant surprise to disembark the ship and be greeted, not with men on horseback, but a grandeur from the city's Spanish and Portuguese history I hadn't expected. I set off exploring on foot down the cobbled lanes near the port with no preconceptions as to what I might find and it wasn't long before I heard drums. I waited to see what would happen and was rewarded a few minutes later by the sight of a large group of people parading down the middle of the street banging out a beat that sounded African in its roots.

The Uruguayan's call it the candombe and it was infectious, prompting those on the sidelines into spontaneous bursts of dancing. I may or may not have kicked my heels up.

An aroma of broiled and barbequing meat hung on the air and I decided to follow my nose. It led me to the Mercado Del Puerto, the undercover port market where the tantalising smells began to mingle with the odour of fish caught from the briny waters of the Rio de la Plato. I was feeling adventurous because I stepped out of my comfort zone to sample a dish called choto, which translates as barbequed lamb tripe. I think perhaps it was a dish that would grow on one but I didn't hang around long enough to find out. Nevertheless, the meal filled the gap and I carried on to the central Plaza Independencia to admire the city's hub before winding my way into the surrounding labyrinth of streets.

It was hot, a sticky close heat akin to how I'd imagine it would be to wade through soup and I was drawn into a bar to enjoy a cold beer while observing the tango being performed. There was something voyeuristic almost in watching the intimacy of the couples dancing and feeling as though I'd intruded, I downed my ale and carried on.

I finished my time ashore with a brisk stroll along the Ramblas, a stretch of continuous avenue running the length of Montevideo's coast. The mighty Atlantic crashed on one side of me and children played football in the green spaces on the other.

I always thought I'd go back there one day, Bronagh, but it wasn't to be. It's a funny thing, you know, because I thought I'd revisit a lot of the places I saw as a young man once I retired but the inclination was gone by the time I was of a pensionable age.

Now then, let's move on to more important matters. I have to say the lemon drizzle cake is the leading contender to date and, as always, I look forward to hearing your verdict on this week's cake.

Yours

Leonard Walsh.

Bronagh sighed feeling as if she'd taken a mini-break to Uruguay's capital. She imagined what it would be like to dance such an intimate dance like the tango. What would it be like to dance it with Leonard? Aisling and Quinn had taken salsa dance classes and look where they'd led. Sure, they'd even performed the Latin American dance at their wedding. Her eyes flicked to the postcard leaning against the computer. There they were now, honeymooning in some unpronounceable place in an igloo! A very posh igloo by all accounts too and they were having a wonderful time gadding about in their padded snow suits. Her mind turned to cake. It never took much turning when it came to cake and she had to agree with Leonard in respect of the lemon drizzle. It was her favourite so far too.

Every Friday on her way home from O'Mara's she'd taken to calling in at the Cherry on Top, cake shop in order to buy herself and her mam a treat to enjoy after their dinner. The clean, sweet tang of fresh baking would tickle her nostrils as she pushed through the door, pausing to admire the array of taste-bud teasing treats on offer in the cabinet. Her mam was partial to New York cheesecake while she was fond of anything with icing and cream. It was on a Friday afternoon too that a sample cake would be placed on the counter for patrons to try a sliver of. When Bronagh had mentioned this in a letter to Leonard, he'd given her the role of chief cake tester. He'd written to say he himself had a sweet tooth and fancied himself a cake connoisseur. He'd been particularly impressed by the gooey chocolate fudge cake he'd enjoyed last time he was in Dublin and was always eager to try the new, and untasted. As such, when he came to visit in September, he'd take Bronagh to the Cherry on Top where he would treat her to a cup of coffee and a wedge of the cake she deemed to be their best. In the weeks since Aisling's wedding, once Moira had hung up her personal trainer cap and the diet was a distance memory, Bronagh had been enjoying her Friday afternoon samplings. To date she'd tried a Cherry on Top's red velvet, angel food, Victoria sponge and of course lemon drizzle cakes. Chief cake tester, was a role Bronagh took seriously.

The door burst open and she forgot all about cakes as Mr and Mrs Blevins from Wales trooped in, carting bags of shopping. Their faces were barely visible inside the hoods of their rain jackets and they stamped their feet on the mat inside the entrance, hastily shutting the door behind them.

'Lovely day for the ducks out there, Bronagh,' Mr Blevins muttered.

'You didn't get too wet, I hope.' She smiled over at them as she folded the letter up and put it back in the envelope. She'd write back on Friday when she'd seen what was on offer at the Cherry on Top this week.

'We're from Wales, Bronagh, we've plenty of happy ducks there too.' Mrs Blevins chuckled.

Chapter 11

MAUREEN KNOCKED ON the door of the white, stone cottage. There was a prickly creeper enveloping one side of it which would be a mass of flowers come summer time. Now though, it was bare and spindly with knobbly buds giving the only clue as to what was to come. She tilted her head to one side to see if she could hear footsteps coming but the only sound was a blackbird warbling in the apple tree over to her right. She knocked again and took a step back wondering whether she should poke her head around the side of the house where she could see a wheelbarrow with a few freshly dug spuds in it. Her tutor might be in the back garden but before she could make her mind up, a woman appeared pulling off the gardening gloves she was wearing.

Maureen knew instantly this was a relationship that was going to work out because Maria de Valera was the image of a singing teacher. Or, at the very least, how Maureen envisaged a singing teacher to look. Her light brown hair was long and left loose, with a few silver threads around the temples streaking through it. She was wearing a cream Aran jumper and a flowing paisley skirt with her feet in a pair wellington boots. Alright the wellington boots weren't part of the music teacher scenario but the woman had obviously been working outside.

She dropped the gloves in the wheelbarrow and held out a hand. 'Hello there. Sorry, I was out the back doing a spot of pruning when I realised what the time was. You must be Maureen, I'm Maria. It's lovely to meet you.'

Oh, yes, Maureen thought, beaming, even her speaking voice had a melodious timbre as she shook her hand enthusiastically. 'I'm looking forward to this, Maria, thank you for fitting me in at such short notice.'

'Not a bother. It was perfect timing in fact, Maureen, given I'd had a cancellation. Right then, come on in.'

Maureen followed behind her wondering whether she should remove her shoes as she watched Maria step out of her wellies, revealing feet clad in woolly brown socks. She'd only walked from the car to the front door not trudged through muddy fields. Maria read her mind. 'Leave them on, Maureen, you're grand. I've the fire on so you won't need your coat. You can hang it there.' She pointed to the hooks on the back of the door as they both stepped into the narrow, dark hallway. Maureen divested herself of her coat and hung it up, breathing in the jostling scents of incense and slow-cooking meat. She was led down the hall to the back of the cottage, spying bedrooms off to the left and the right. The light and airy living space she found herself in looked out onto an expansive back garden with more fruit trees and several raised vegetable beds. The area was enclosed by a brick wall. The additional room was a pleasant surprise given the age of the front of the cottage.

'An extension,' Maria said, registering Maureen's expression as she looked around. 'Best thing we ever did.'

'It's a lovely room, looking out on your garden like so. Do you grow your own vegetables?' Maureen gestured to the raised beds where she could see all sorts of leafy greens on the go.

'Yes, we do. I'm a big believer in you are what you eat.'

That would make her a digestive biscuit then, Maureen thought, impressed by Maria's prowess in the garden. She'd struggled to keep the potted begonia Rosemary Farrell had bought her for her birthday alive. It had been touch and go on several occasions when the plant had looked like it was on its last legs but she'd had a word with Him upstairs and like a miracle it had always rallied. She'd never hear the end of it if it died. It was the first thing Rosemary looked for whenever she called in.

The open plan area they were standing in had a modest but functional kitchen in the corner and the rest of the floorspace was given over to an overstuffed blue sofa with a throw rug tossed over its arm. Bean bags were strewn on the floor along with scatter cushions and a veritable symphony of musical instruments including a piano. An enormous book case dominated one side of the wall space. It was overflowing with dusty old tomes. There was no television Maureen realised soaking it all up. She couldn't imagine not having a tele. 'Do you play all of these?' She made a sweeping arc at the instruments with her hand.

Maria laughed. 'No, I sing and play piano. My husband plays the guitar and our oldest is learning the flute; our middle child's keen on the violin and Jessie the baby she likes the tambourine and castanets.'

'What a clever lot you are.' Maureen was delighted by the thought of this musical family getting up from the table each night after dinner to bond over their instruments. How lovely. Her lot had fought over what programme they were going to watch on the idiot box and whose turn it was to help with the washing-up. She sighed. She'd have loved it if they could have all harmonised together, a family brought together by their music. Ha, no show! There was Aisling not even able to get a place in the children's choir at St Theresa's. She'd even resorted to bribery in the form of one of her famous porter cakes but the choirmaster would not be bought. As for music, her head ached at the memory of the awful stuff that had come blaring out of their bedrooms. The number of times she'd had to remind them they lived on the top floor of a guesthouse and the people paying good money to be in the rooms below did not want to be subjected to Def Tiger and Twisted Brother or the like.

Patrick had been the biggest offender, him and that ghetto blaster of his. She shuddered, recalling how he'd grown his hair long and had it permed. That wasn't the worst of it though. Oh no, the leather pants he'd squeezed himself into were an abomination. She'd told him until she was blue in the face his bits and bobs wouldn't be able to breathe through all that leather. Sure, she'd said, he'd ruin his chances at fathering a family. And look, here he was now, a man closer to forty than thirty with no children. A mammy knew best. She shook the image of Patrick in his teens away, envisaging a happier scene whereby the O'Maras were gathered in the family's living room having a jam session or whatever you called it. She blinked, realising she'd just pictured the Partridge Family.

'Are you alright there, Maureen. You look a little pale. Would you like a glass of water before we begin?'

'No, thank you.' Maureen gathered herself. She was paying by the hour. It was time to get this show on the road.

Maria gestured towards the piano and sat down on the stool before lifting the lid. She pushed her hair back over her shoulders and then flexed her fingers. Maureen wasn't sure where to put herself. She didn't want to lean over the piano like some sort of saloon girl but she felt a little eejitty standing there with nothing to do with her hands. 'Maria, would your little one mind if I borrowed her tambourine for the lesson?'

Maria looked surprised. 'We're going to be doing scales, Maureen, and I'll be showing you some breathing exercises which will help free your voice. I'm not sure you're going to need a tambourine.'

'It's just that I'd feel more comfortable with something in my hands.'

'Oh, I see. You don't need to be nervous with me but if it helps, I'm sure Jessie won't mind. Help yourself.'

Maureen retrieved the plastic tambourine and her shoulders relaxed as she stood alongside the piano. She gave it a rattle for good measure. 'Sorry,' she said to Maria whose fingers had been about to strike the keys. 'Do you happen to know any Fleetwood Mac? Your Stevie one was very good on the tambourine. You've the look of her, you know.'

'No, I can't say I've had much call to play Fleetwood Mac, Maureen. My pupils tend to want to sing Barbara Streisand, Bette Midler, Celine Dion that sort of thing.'

'Not me. Not my cup of tea at all. I'm like that song, you know the one. I'm a little bit country and a little bit rock 'n' roll.' She shook the tambourine for effect.

'Yes, you told me on the telephone when you booked that you're going to be singing in a country band.'

'I am. Do you happen to know any Dolly Parton or Sheena Easton? Because I've to sing *Islands in the Stream* and *We've Got Tonight*.'

'I'd have to hunt some sheet music down but we're getting ahead of ourselves Maureen. We're going to start in middle C and run through Do-Re-Mi-Fa-So-La-Ti-Do like this.

Maria sang the scale and Maureen nodded. 'You've very good pitch.'

'Thank you. I want to hear you do it now. On the count of three here we go. One, two, three and...'

Maureen sang the ditty then looked to Maria to see what she had to say.

'It was very hard to hear you over the tambourine, Maureen. Do you think we could run through it again without it this time?'

'I didn't even realise I was shaking it.' Maureen laughed, looking at the instrument in her hand as though she'd had no part in rattling it.

Maria smiled and took a deep breath. 'Okay, so again on the count of three.'

As Maureen tapped the tambourine against her thigh, Maria thought to herself, it was going to be a very long hour indeed.

Chapter 12

MAUREEN WAS PRACTISING her scales as she set about prepping the vegetables to go with her roasted salmon in lemon butter sauce. Maria had given her a practise CD and she was a committed student. Pooh was watching her quizzically from his basket. She'd had words with him earlier. He was to be on his best behaviour this evening or there'd be ructions because Donal was coming to dinner. She glanced at the wall clock. Aisling should be home anytime now, she thought and on cue the telephone rang.

'Mammy, we're home,' Aisling gushed.

'Is that you, Aisling?'

'Who else has been away, Mammy?'

'Don't be clever with me and welcome home! I got your postcard and it sounded like you were enjoying yourselves. Did you write to Quinn's mammy and daddy too?'

'I did.'

'How many postcards did you send them because I'm only after getting the one.'

'I sent one each to all our friends and family. I didn't have time for writing any more than that. I was on my honeymoon, remember.'

Maureen was appeased. 'Did you have a lovely time?'

'Ah, we did, Mammy, it was wonderful. It was a fairyland so it was. I've hundreds of photos to show you.'

'I'm looking forward to seeing them. How's Quinn?'

'My husband, you mean?'

Moira yelled out in the background, 'Mammy, she's driving me mad saying that. Tell her to stop.'

'How long have you been home?'

'Half an hour.'

Maureen shook her head; she'd bang their heads together if she was there.

'Quinn's got a cold, Mammy.'

'I'm not surprised, given you've been honeymooning in the Arctic. What do you expect, getting up to shenanigans in the freezing cold?'

'Mammy, what's that music?'

'Oh, it's the piano scales. I'm after starting singing lessons.'

'Why?'

Maureen's nose grew as she said, 'Because, Aisling, I've decided to use the voice the good Lord saw fit to give me. I'd forgotten what a joy it is to sing but the karaoke on your hen night brought it back to me.'

Aisling sniggered down the line at the memory of her mammy prancing about on stage with her skirt tucked in her knickers.

'Has your sister told you about the yoga pants party I'm after having next week?'

'She mentioned something about a Tupperware party.'

'It's not Tupperware it's yoga pants, I've told Moira a hundred times. That girl's ears are painted on.'

'Where did she get Tupperware from then?'

'Because it's like a Tupperware party only we'll be selling yoga pants and I expect it to be a family effort, Aisling.'

'Mammy, I'm lost. I don't see the connection between the two.'

Maureen rolled her eyes. 'Never mind, just be sure to pencil in next Saturday.'

'I will. Bronagh said everything ticked over smoothly while I was away. She seemed a little preoccupied though, Mammy.'

'Did she? I saw her earlier in the week and she was grand. Her mam's having a good spell. Bronagh's probably on another diet. You know what she gets like.'

'You're probably right.'

'I went to see a good film yesterday called *Castoff*. It was about Tom Hanks and a coconut he made friends with.'

'Sounds riveting, Mammy. Who'd you go with?'

'My friend Donal.' She remembered her promise to Donal to pin Aisling down for a date when she got home so he could arrange the lunch he had planned. 'And listen, for some mad reason he wants to meet you and your sisters. Roisin, as my official yoga pants supplier, is coming over next weekend, Noah's at his fathers. So, how're you fixed for a Sunday pub lunch at Johnnie Fox's? His two daughters will be there too and, Aisling, don't be going on to Moira about it either. I'll have a quiet word with her.'

Maureen heard a frenzied whispering and the next thing Moira came on the phone. 'So, we're finally going to meet this Donal fella then.'

'He's not 'this Donal fella' he's Donal, thank you very much. And you are to behave yourself next Sunday. I've not met his two girls yet and I don't want you showing me up,' she said, repeating another version of what she'd said to Pooh earlier. 'And you're not to be wearing anything that shows your knickers either. Do you hear me?'

'I hear you. Mammy?'

'What is it?'

'Before you go, can you tell Aisling her and Quinn aren't to be carrying on in the bedroom with me next door.'

Maureen frowned. 'I will not. She's a ring on her finger, she's perfectly entitled to be carrying on, unlike some I could mention.'

'Mammy it is not 1950.'

Maureen spied the spuds boiling over. She'd no time for getting into a morals debate with her youngest child, and she said goodbye in time to Do-Re-Mi-Fa-So-La-Ti-Do in ascending C major.

Chapter 13

MAUREEN HAD THE MEAL she was preparing for her and Donal as ready as it could be without actually dishing it up when she heard his knock on the door. She gave her hands a quick wash and dried them on her apron, remembering to take it off before she made her way to the door. She hadn't spent all that time agonising over what to wear, finally settling on her yoga pants so as she'd be relaxed, teemed with a deep pink sweater she knew looked well on her, to cover it up with her shamrock pinny. She flung the door open with a sense of anticipation as to the evening ahead and there he was with a bottle of wine in one hand and a bunch of roses which he thrust out toward her in the other. She took the flowers from him, thinking he looked very handsome tonight in his blue shirt and dress jeans.

'They're gorgeous but you shouldn't of, Donal,' she said, burying her nose in their soft petals and inhaling the heady perfume. She was very glad he had, though.

'The florist told me pink symbolises grace and elegance which I told her was perfect for the lady I was presenting them to. They smell lovely too but not as lovely as you. I've a soft spot for that Arpège of yours.'

'You're very kind.' Maureen turned as pink as her roses. She stepped aside and gestured for him to come in. 'C'mon now and make yourself at home.'

Donal stepped over the threshold, scanning the room for Pooh the way a person in the wilderness would keep a wary eye out for grizzly bears. The poodle was sitting in his basket and if it were possible for him to have a sulky look on his little poodly face he would have. He eyeballed Donal as though sizing him up for dinner and Maureen followed his gaze.

'Ah now, don't you worry about him. I've gotten the hang of the positive reinforcement so I have and he knows which side his bread is buttered on.'

Donal chuckled moving into the living room. 'I'll take your word for it.' He addressed Pooh. 'Hello, boy. How're you doing?'

Pooh gave a woof and Maureen exclaimed, 'There you go he said hello. He's very clever, you know.' She bustled into the kitchen, putting the flowers down on the worktop while she retrieved a doggy treat. Consistency was the key.

Donal wasn't so sure, it was hello. He thought it more likely to be a 'feck off away with you' but he didn't say anything. He sized the dog up and decided giving him a pat might be pushing the boundaries of their tenuous relationship.

'There you go, Pooh. See? Nice things happen when you're a good boy.' Maureen held out her hand so he could snaffle his reward.

Donal began to relax now he was sure he wasn't going to be mauled and took a moment to look about the room. He'd been here before, but just the once and not for long, when he'd picked Maureen up to take her for a country drive. 'You have it lovely, Maureen. It's you to a T.'

'Thank you. It took a while for this place to feel like home. It was such a change from O'Mara's but it's home now alright.'

His gaze swung to the array of ornaments decorating a wall shelf, one in particular, and he crossed the room to take a closer look. 'This is unusual, do you mind me asking what it is?'

'Not at all.' Although Maureen thought it was self-evident. 'That, is a canoe.'

'A canoe you say?' Donal eyed the phallic-shaped wooden creation on the shelf with a raised eyebrow. 'Ah yes, now I can see it. I didn't twig because there aren't any oars.'

'I carved it myself in a small village in Vietnam on the holiday I was after telling you about with Moira. I wouldn't fancy my chances at carving the fiddly little oars. I'd have probably taken a finger off.'

'You're a woman full of surprises, Maureen.'

Maureen was pleased he found her mysterious. She'd always wanted to be mysterious and wasn't it a bonus he found her so when she wasn't even wearing her mammy of the bride hat?

'Whatever you've got cooking smells wonderful.'

'I hope you like fish?'

'I love fish which is why I suggested Johnnie Fox's for our family get together; the seafood is delicious there.'

'I'm glad to hear it because we're having roasted salmon in lemon butter with mashed potatoes and seasonal vegetables.' Maureen liked saying seasonal vegetables. It sounded far more interesting than green beans and broccoli. She remembered the flowers and located a vase in her cabinet that would do nicely to display them in. As she was titivating the roses, Donal put the wine he'd brought down beside her and suggested he open it to allow it to breathe.

'You'll find the corkscrew there in the top drawer and I thought I'd leave it to you to choose some music.'

Donal tended to the wine and then searched through Maureen's CDs settling on Fleetwood Mac which led to Maureen telling him all about the singing lessons she'd taken it upon herself to have. 'I want my voice in tip-top condition for the party in Clontarf. We'll be rehearsing beforehand I hope.'

'The boys and I were talking about getting together to practise next Saturday afternoon. You could come along to that if you like.'

'Ah, no, I can't. Rosi's coming over from London and we're holding a yoga pants party.' She explained the premise and breathed a sigh of relief he didn't get all muddled with the Tupperware side of things. 'I wondered if the Sunday would work for you and your girls to have lunch, what with Rosi being here too.'

'That sounds a grand idea. Leave it with me and I'll check with Anna and Louise tomorrow and get back to you. We could have a practice ourselves tonight after dinner if you like. I saw your Kenny Roger's CDs.'

'I'd like that.'

Maureen had set the table earlier and Donal did the honours, lighting the candle and pouring the wine while she plated their meals.

There was no shortage of conversation over dinner as he told her about the job he'd done this week for a woman whose wiring needed replacing because a family of mice had chewed their way through it in her attic. Maureen resolved to be nice to Peaches next door; she might come in handy. She in turn told him about her line dancing and after they'd carried their plates through to the kitchen, Donal asked if she could teach him one of the dances to work off his dinner before they had dessert.

'The boot scootin boogie is an easy one but we'll need the right music. I've a Billy Ray Cyrus CD there somewhere.'

Donal sorted their sounds and Maureen talked him through the steps overtop of the music. 'Step right to side and cross left behind, touch left heel diagonally, forward and clap.' She clapped.

Donal who had the wrong foot forward laughed and asked if they could start over. They did so and he was no better the second time around which set Maureen off giggling. 'I'm afraid you're no Billy Ray.'

'Two left feet.' He grinned. 'Go on you show me how it's done.'

Maureen demonstrated the dance and he clapped along giving her a round of applause when she'd finished. She took a bow and announced it was time for dessert. She'd caught her breath by the time she placed the dishes of chocolate mousse down on the table. Donal topped their glasses up with the remains of the red.

'This is going down a treat, Maureen,' Donal said, in between spoonfuls of the mousse.

Maureen was pleased with how rich and creamy it had turned out and had to agree it was going down nicely.

They'd polished off the wine and Donal had all but licked his bowl when they decided it was time to get around to the business of rehearsing.

'We need a microphone each if we're to make it feel authentic,' Maureen stated. She was in a giggly mood which was down to Donal and the wine. Her cheeks too were feeling a little hot as she disappeared into the kitchen, ignoring the detritus left behind from dinner as she retrieved a whisk and a wooden spoon. 'Here we are, you can have the whisk. I'm quite at home with the wooden spoon.' She'd chased her children around the kitchen often enough with it when they were younger. Donal had the music poised to go and he aimed the remote. The opening notes drifted into the room and Pooh gave a happy sigh as he settled down for some Kenny and a snooze.

Donal had a lovely voice; it was gruff and gravely and sounded very like the man himself, Maureen thought, as she did each time she heard him sing. She was so engrossed in listening to him she nearly missed her opening and came in a little wobbly but found her feet and sang her heart out, all the while losing herself in those grey twinkling eyes of Donal's. They were serenading one another she realised and when the song finished, he took her in his arms kissing her slowly and what happened next was the most natural thing in the world.

Chapter 14

MOIRA AND AISLING BANGED on the apartment door. They'd decided to surprise their mammy by taking her out for morning tea. It was a bright and sunny winter's day, perfect for a spot of Howth people-watching over an oversized cookie and cup of coffee. Aisling was itching to tell her mammy all about her holiday, too.

'Mammy,' Moira put her mouth near the door and called out. Her dark hair fell across her face and she nearly toppled into her mammy as the door swung open. Maureen poked her head around it.

'Would you stop your hollering, the neighbours will be after complaining.'

She was belting her dressing gown up, Moira's eagle eye noticed and her hair was tousled.

'You're up late, Mammy. That's not like you.' Aisling leaned in to kiss her on the cheek. It was warm and soft and there was the faintest whiff of Arpège. 'Moira and I thought we'd take you out for morning coffee. I've loads to tell you about Jukkasjarvi. But we can't very well go out with you in your dressing gown.' It was a puzzle. Mammy was usually up and dressed by sparrow's fart.

'Yuckisvari is the place where the Ice Hotel is and she hasn't stopped going on about it since she got back,' Moira explained. 'And she's doing my head in with her 'my husband' business. You want to hear her, Mammy. This morning she said to me, "pass me the milk because my husband likes his tea milky in the morning."' Moira made a gagging noise.

Aisling scowled at her sister. 'Well, he is my husband.'

'Yes, he is, Aisling, we're all aware of that fact given we were there when you said your vows. It's lovely of you girls to think of your mammy and come by too. Aisling, I have to say you're looking very well on it given you've been in the Arctic. You've a rosy glow to your cheeks.'

'That's nothing to do with the Arctic, that's the riding. Mammy, I can't cope. I thought the headboard was going to come through the wall last night.'

Aisling shoved her elbow in her sister's ribs and while Moira was doubled over, Maureen announced her plan. 'Now then, here's what we'll do. How about you both head on down to that lovely coffee shop near the pier. The one that does the enormous cookies you're both so fond of. I'll make myself presentable and meet you there in fifteen minutes or so. You could take him with you if you like.' Pooh had appeared at her side having heard the sisters' voices. He was trying to push his way out the door so he could receive the attention he felt was his due having been ignored for the best part of the evening before.

Moira eyed her mammy; she was behaving oddly. Something was up.

Aisling stared at her mammy. She was being furtive. Something wasn't right.

'No, you're grand, Mammy. We don't mind waiting here while you get dressed.' Moira had decided enough was enough, she'd find out first-hand what was going on and she made to bypass Maureen. Her mammy moved with lightning speed for someone of her age, Moira thought as she blocked the entrance. Oh yes, something was definitely up. She had a nose for knowing when things weren't right. 'Mammy, what are you doing? Let me in.'

'Ah no, Moira, the place is a mess. You don't need to be coming in. Sure, head on down to the café like I said. I'll be there soon.' She tried to shut the door, wincing as a cough sounded from somewhere inside and both Moira and Aisling's eyes bugged as the realisation their mammy was not alone dawned.

Moira stuck her foot in the door and her voice came out in a strangled whisper. 'I knew you were up to something. Have you your man friend in there?'

Maureen bit her bottom lip.

'You have too,' Aisling said. 'I know that look. It's the same one you get when you don't want to own up to eating the last snowball.'

'Or, when you steal my clothes,' Moira muttered.

'Come on now, girls, we're all adults here, let's be reasonable.'

'I'm not. I'm the baby of the family,' Moira said, bottom lip firmly out as her voice ramped up several notches.

'Moira, you're twenty-six.'

'And you're my mammy and mammies don't go riding their man friends on a Friday night!'

Aisling put her hands over her ears. She felt like sitting down on the floor and rocking back and forth. She was the one who'd just been on her honeymoon. She was the newlywed; as such it should be her and her husband getting up to shenanigans. Not Mammy!

'Moira, would you keep it down. I've an elderly woman across the way who doesn't need to be hearing you giving out about my private business.'

'So, you're not denying it then. You've done the deed,' Moira stated, not in the least contrite as she peered past her mammy trying to catch a glimpse of this Donal fella.

Maureen danced about like Rocky Balboa, trying to block her view.

'Mammy, you can't blame Moira for being upset. It's hard getting used to the idea of you with someone who isn't Daddy,' Aisling said, mercifully keeping her voice down.

'How do you think I'm finding it?' Maureen hissed back, feeling close to tears. This was not how she'd thought her morning would go. She'd envisaged a cooked breakfast then her and Donal would read the papers and after that perhaps take Pooh for a walk along the pier. No, being shouted at by her youngest child and stared at by her middle daughter as though she'd committed a heinous crime hadn't been on her agenda when she'd opened her eyes and seen Donal smiling at her. 'You're being very selfish the pair of you. Off you go now. I'll see you in the café shortly.' She hauled Pooh in by the collar and shut the door in their surprised faces.

Donal was dressed and sitting on the end of the bed, bent over as he put his shoes on, when she went back into the bedroom.

'Did you hear all that?'

He straightened and nodded as he looked at her. 'I did, and I'm sorry I've put you in an awkward position with your girls. I'll head off home and let you sort things out with them.'

'I don't want you to go and it's not your fault, Donal. It's those two behaving like children but I should go and talk to them.' They'd both be getting a flea in their ear when she joined them. 'I said I'd meet them down the road at a café there but can I at least make you a cup of tea and some toast before you go.'

He stood up and wrapped her in an embrace, planting a kiss on top of her head. 'You go and talk to your girls. I'll get on home and call you later to see how it went. Our children are always our children, Maureen, and they need to know you're still their mammy no matter what else is going on in your life.'

Maureen decided she was definitely falling in love with Donal McArthy because, unlike her offspring, he was a kind and tolerant man. She saw him to the door and then spent a rushed ten minutes showering and tidying herself up before rounding up Pooh and heading down to meet Aisling and Moira.

Chapter 15

THE DAY WAS INDEED glorious, Maureen thought, wishing her mood matched the bright weather as she weaved her way down the busy main street. You'd almost get away with no coat if you stayed on the sunny side of the road. She said hello to a man whose name eluded her but whom she knew through the yacht club before settling Pooh down outside the café. 'We'll go for a lovely walk along the pier once I've sorted those two eejits sitting inside there out. You be a good boy, now.' She handed him a treat and once satisfied he was happy to sit observing the foot traffic, giving the odd conversational yap, she gave him a final pat and pushed the door open.

The coffee shop was buzzing with chatter and the clatter of cups and saucers. The air thick with ground beans and cinnamon. Aisling and Moira were sitting at a table dappled with sunshine, in the corner of the nautical-themed space. Her eyes narrowed seeing Aisling was talking to someone on her mobile. She'd put money on it being Roisin. They'd already ordered, she also saw, noticing Moira was nursing a cup of coffee. There was an oversized chocolate chip cookie in front of her. The tell-tale crumbs on the plate in front of Aisling told her it would take more than her mammy having her man friend stay overnight to put her off her food. She joined the short line waiting to be served.

MOIRA HAD TELEPHONED Roisin as soon as she'd gotten her backside down on a seat inside the café, her hot chocolate and cookie untouched as she hit speed dial for her sister. It would give her something to do while they waited for Mammy to put in an appearance. Her head was not in a good space because she'd almost told the chap with the bandana tied around his head, pirate style, who'd taken her order, to feck off away with himself when he'd greeted her with an 'ahoy there, me hearty, and what can I get for you today?' She could not find a correlation between cappuccino and pirates nor was she in the mood to.

When Roisin heard the breaking news coming out of Howth, she'd been taken aback. This was not a conversation she'd been expecting to have as she enjoyed a lazy Saturday morning eating her cornflakes and glancing over the paper. 'Are you sure? How do you know, anyway? Noah stop running that car up and down the mat for one minute, please! I can't hear myself think.'

'I'm positive and Aisling can confirm it.' Moira held the phone out and Aisling leaned in and said, 'Affirmative.'

Moira carried on, 'See. Aisling and I dropped in on Mammy unexpectedly this morning because we were going to take her out for morning coffee and when she opened the door, she wasn't dressed.'

'Jaysus feck! Are you telling me she was naked when she opened the door?'

'Rosi! Is Noah in the room with you?'

'No, he's gone into his bedroom but I thought you just said Mammy was naked when she opened the door this morning?'

'No, Rosi, you eejit. You're as sharp as a beach ball some-times. She had her dressing gown on but she was more than likely naked under that.'

Roisin dropped the spoon back in her bowl. She'd lost her appetite.

'She was acting awfully cagey, you know the way she does when she's up to something and then we heard a cough and we knew.'

'Who coughed?'

'Rosi, keep up! Her man friend of course. He was in the apartment and our mammy was naked under her dressing gown which means they weren't playing fecking Monopoly.'

An older woman looked over the rim of her cup at them, eyes popping, as did several other diners, their ears burning.

Aisling held her finger up to her mouth to shush her sister, thinking for all they knew they may well have been playing the game. She and Quinn had a game of strip Monopoly one evening and very good fun it had been, too.

'Where are you now?' Roisin asked.

'At the café waiting for Mammy to show herself.'

Roisin frowned. She sounded as if she expected her to ap-pear wearing a scarlet letter A. 'Don't be giving out to her, Moira. I know it's hard to get used to the idea of her being with anyone else.'

'Wrong is what it is,' Moira butted in.

'No, you're being over the top. It's hard alright, Moira, but she's entitled to a life and we have to accept that.'

'Easy for you to say over in London. It wasn't you confront-ed with a naked Mammy.'

'She was in her dressing gown.' Roisin tried to calm her sister. 'She loved Daddy. You know that.'

Moira scuffed at the vinyl flooring with the toe of her trainer. 'Yes but—'

'There isn't a but. She did and we know he's not here anymore so we're all going to have to accept Mammy has a boyfriend.'

'Man friend,' Moira corrected, sniffing.

'Put Aisling on, would you?'

'Hello,' Aisling said a second later.

'Will you not talk some sense into her?'

'I'm trying to but you know what Moira's like. She can be a right gobshite sometimes.'

Moira pulled a face at her sister.

'But I won't give Mammy a hard time and neither will she.' She glared at Moira. 'Or, I'll put the boot in under the table. She's here!' Aisling spotted her in the queue. 'Got to go.' She ended the call and handed the phone back to Moira before pushing her chair back and standing up. 'We said we'd treat her.'

'Well don't look at me. I'm the poor student, remember,' Moira said, not budging.

'Sure, you're tighter than a camel's hole in a sandstorm these days.'

'I'm not tight, Aisling. I don't have money to be throwing around is all.'

Aisling shook her head; she couldn't be bothered arguing. She went to stand alongside her mammy. 'What are you wanting, Mammy? I'll order it for you if you like. You go and sit down.'

'No, I'll not be beholden to you, Aisling O'Mara,' Maureen said with a wounded air before inching forward in the line.

Aisling knew there was no placating her when she was in wronged mammy mode so she left her to it.

Five minutes later Maureen, carrying her still warm, double chocolate cookie over to the table along with the number for her drink order, sat down. It was a funny thing. She'd noticed several of the patrons glance at her as she passed by their tables and fancied it was admiration she was seeing on their faces. She'd have wondered if she'd managed to get her skirt caught up in her knickers again if she hadn't of been wearing her yoga pants. She fixed her youngest child with a stare that would bring a grown man to his knees. 'Moira O'Mara, I'd like you to apologise to me for your earlier rant. I was scarlet so I was. Sure, half of Howth would have heard you giving out.'

Moira refused to meet her mammy's gaze as she squirmed uncomfortably in her seat.

'Do ya hear me?'

'Yes. I'm sorry, Mammy,' she mumbled, her dark hair hiding her face.

'What was that, I can't hear you?'

'I'm sorry.' She looked up, her eyes a little too bright, 'It was a shock was all.'

'And you, what have you to say for yourself?' She turned her attention to Aisling.

'I'm sorry too, Mammy, but Moira's right, it was the shock.'

'Oh, the shock was it?' Maureen hit the high notes. 'And how do you think I felt when you announced you were wanting to marry that Jackeen Marcus, or you,' she pointed to Moira. 'Fraternising with a married man. The shame of it.'

There was steam coming out of the ears of the diners at the surrounding tables. You couldn't pay for entertainment this good!

'Mammy, lower your voice, you're getting hysterical,' Aisling whispered, her face puce as she saw people staring over.

'I miss Daddy, Mammy.' Moira sniffed not caring who saw as a tear streaked down her cheek.

The wind went out of Maureen's sails. 'I know you do. We all do.'

Aisling dropped an arm around her sister and Moira leaned into her.

'Can you not try and understand. I've been lonely and what a tonic it's been for me meeting Donal?'

'I do understand.' Moira's voice wobbled. She was tired of being angry and knew what lay at the root of it all. 'I'm sorry, Mammy. I know I'm being selfish. I can't help it but I feel like I'm being disloyal to Daddy if I pretend I'm happy about you and this Donal fella.'

'It's Donal not this Donal fella, Moira, as I keep telling you and I know you do.' Maureen reached across the table and patted her daughter's hand. 'Because I struggled with those feeling myself but your daddy wouldn't want me to be lonely, Moira. He was a kind man and he didn't have a selfish bone in his body. Do you remember what he told us about how he wanted us to look after one another when he was gone and how we needed to find our way without him the best we could, which is what I'm trying to do.'

Moira looked at her mammy, tears clinging to her lashes.

'All I'm asking, Moira, is for you to keep an open mind where Donal's concerned.'

'I'll try,' Moira said, taking the serviette from Maureen and dabbing her eyes.

'And you too.' Maureen turned to Aisling who nodded.

The clearing of a throat made them all look up. The pirate man from behind the counter was standing there with Maureen's cappuccino.

Chapter 16

BRONAGH WAS ENJOYING her Saturday morning. She'd allowed herself a sleep in until past eight o'clock, a luxury not available Monday to Friday and had gotten up to make a leisurely breakfast of toast and eggs for her and Mam. Now she was sitting at the kitchen table, her back being warmed by the rays of sunlight flooding into the room as she penned her letter to Leonard. It was a newsy update as she wrote about the upcoming yoga pants party and the taster of carrot cake with thick cream cheese icing she'd made short work of on her way home last night. She'd thought the lemon drizzle hard to beat but there was something about that cream cheese icing and the way it offset the sweetness of the cake. It was delicious, she scribbled. Given she was a cream and icing sort of a girl, she was putting this high praise of the carrot cake down to the mix of cream cheese and icing sugar.

Her mam was in the living room, industriously arts and crafting with her scrapbook along with her old pal Linda. She'd been bright lately which lifted Bronagh's spirits and today Linda had called in to see her with a bag full of odds and sods with which to decorate their various projects. Linda was working on a doll-size book for her great granddaughter who'd entered the world a month ago, while Myrna's was a keepsake of memories from when she and Hilary were small.

Myrna had known Linda since before Hilary was born. They'd worked together at Arnotts, her mam in the millinery department, Linda behind the counter in children's wear. They were busy snipping and pasting photographs and cardboard embellishments at this very moment and Bronagh could hear them laughing. She imagined it to be over some memory an old photo of Myrna's had evoked. She put the pen down as she remembered another time when her mam had been laughing along with Linda in the front room.

1971

'I'm off now.' Bronagh stuck her head around the living room door where she saw her mam sitting in the armchair, warming her feet by the gas fire. Linda, her friend from her Arnotts days, was opposite her in her mam's old chair, her toes vying for space. They were reminiscing over their days behind the counter at the department store, both grinning like Cheshire cats at the laughs they'd had when their floor manager's back was turned. 'The dinner only needs warming through when you're ready,' she said. It was only early but she wasn't going to be home for her tea so she'd made stew and dumplings which could be reheated. Linda who'd arrived an hour or so ago had said she was happy to stay and have her dinner with Myrna which pleased Bronagh. She didn't like the idea of her mam eating on her own.

'That perfume's lovely.' Myrna sniffed. 'Is it new?'

'It is. It's called Rive Gauche, Mam. It's French.' Bronagh breathed, 'French' with reverence. She hoped she hadn't been too heavy handed with it. She'd done what the woman behind the perfume counter had said. She'd sprayed a cloud in the air and walked into it, feeling misty droplets settle over her. It would have mellowed by the time she got to Grafton Street. She'd splurged on the fragrance, having fallen in love with the modern blue canister and the way the scent made her feel like a woman about town. There was something so glamorous about French perfume. Look at Maureen O'Mara; she always smelled gorgeous with her Arpège.

'Let's have a look at you,' Linda said, the slice of thickly buttered brack Bronagh had put out for their afternoon tea halfway to her mouth. 'I like seeing you young one's fashions.'

Bronagh stepped into the room to show off her trouser suit.

'Is that new too, Bronagh?' her mam asked, taking in her daughter's lilac tunic with its tie belt and matching trousers. 'I always liked you in lilac. It's very smart, so.'

Bronagh felt a bit of a spendthrift, especially given they could do with a new toaster; the other had packed up the other week leaving the singed smell of burnt toast in its wake for days after. She didn't treat herself often though and sure, they'd been making do with the grill. There was something about the fella she was going to meet this evening, something special, and whatever it was that got her pulse racing whenever she thought about him, also had her wanting to look her best. She'd decided the toaster could wait. 'Thanks, Mam. It is new. I bought it in the sales this week.'

'The Arnotts sales, I hope,' Linda sniffed.

'Of course.' Bronagh hadn't but they didn't need to know that.

'Did you buy the top and the trousers separately because you've matched the colour ever so well?' Linda gave her a slow and approving head-to-toe appraisal over the top of her glasses.

'No. They were sold together as an outfit.' She'd been pleased with her find, having decided the moment she saw it on the rack it was perfect for a date at Captain America's. She loved the restaurant with its casual but buzzy atmosphere that made you feel you were where it was at. She'd been pleased when Kevin had suggested it. As she thought of how she'd be seeing him again in under an hour, her heart skipped a beat and she hoped she didn't have a silly telltale smile on her face like the one she'd been wearing all week since he'd asked her out. Maureen had been trying to coax out of her what it was had her smiling away like the cat who got the cream all week but she hadn't said a word. She didn't want to tell anyone she was going on a proper date tonight for fear it would jinx things.

'Are you off somewhere special?' Myrna looked hopeful and it tugged at Bronagh. She knew her mam struggled with being dependant on her daughter more and more as her health continued to deteriorate. Her good spells were briefer and the bad spells longer and it all a medical mystery. She was always urging Bronagh to get out and about, meet up with friends. Telling her she was too young to be sitting in with her old mam. She'd insist she enjoyed her own company and sure, didn't she have her crafts to keep her busy? That was true enough. She was currently knitting hats for Hilary's children, when her hands would do what she wanted them to do and she could summon the energy to make the needles clack.

Bronagh would respond by asking her who it was cuddled her when she was small and frightened by the shadows on her bedroom floor? Who'd cleaned up after her when she'd been sick? Who dried her tears and kissed her grazes making them better? Who was it had cooked for her night after night? Who'd sat and listened to her stories when she got home from school of an afternoon? Who sewed her dresses? The list went on and on and she'd always finish by telling her mam it was a privilege to share her meals with the woman who'd done all of that for her.

'BRONAGH?' MYRNA ASKED, seeing the faraway expression on her daughter's face.

'Captain America's, Mam.' She didn't want to say who she was meeting, not in front of Linda because she'd be in for a grilling if she mentioned having been asked out by a fella. She liked Linda; she was loyal, especially when it came to her friendship with Mam but she was also a gossip and the news Bronagh may be courting would be considered the juiciest of information.

Linda sniffed. 'My Lizzie said they're after charging thirty-eight pence for a bun burger. Daylight robbery in my opinion. And why we need to be pretending we're in an American diner when we're Irish I don't know.'

Bronagh smiled. She didn't think Linda would understand it wasn't about the bun burger or what it cost. It wasn't about pretending to be Americans either. It was the *experience*. The sense of being somewhere different as the energy of the place washed over you, the humming conversations, shouts of laughter, clinking glasses and strumming guitar, they all made her forget her responsibilities as she let her hair down and enjoyed the freedom of being young and out on the town. Not to mention their deep-dish apple pie being well worth a trip into the city.

'I'm going to head on now. I don't want to miss my bus.'

'Bronagh, you didn't tell me who you're meeting,' Myrna called after her.

'A friend, Mam,' Bronagh called back ambiguously as she opened the front door, eager to be off before any more questions came her way.

She heard Linda's voice as she made to close the door behind her, 'It's a shame isn't it, Myrna? Your Bronagh not having met anyone. How's Hilary getting on?' Her tread was heavy as walked to the bus stop. It was unnerving to know she was thought of as a spinster and she wasn't even twenty-five yet. She'd been tempted to poke her head back in the door and shout to Linda Carlisle that she was off to meet a very eligible young fella so stick that on your brack and eat it! By the time she clambered aboard the bus and paid her fare, she'd shaken off the remark because nothing was going to spoil her evening.

The bus was nearly full but Bronagh managed to find a seat near the back by the window, her Rive Gauche ensuring she had a seat to herself. The bus driver had been very bold, giving her a wink when she boarded, but she decided it was confirmation she'd chosen well with the lilac trouser suit. She sat with her bag perched on her lap as the double-decker rumbled its way into the city. The street lights blinked on and the dull dusk light faded. She checked her hair in the reflection of the dusty window. She'd put it up and the style had required numerous bobby pins and spray and she was pleased to see it was holding, despite the wind outside's best efforts. Then she turned her mind to Kevin, allowing herself the luxury of conjuring him up as the bus shuddered to a stop to let more passengers on and off.

His skin was smooth and clean shaven with a slight pocking around his cheeks which didn't detract in the least from his easy, languid attractiveness. He was tanned too despite the heat of summer being long gone and his ears poked out from tousled dark hair doing its best to hide them. This was due to his unconscious habit of running his fingers through his hair constantly. His eyes were heavy lidded and blackened and his smile hinted at a cheeky sense of humour. He was what the magazines would call a heartthrob.

By the time she stepped off the bus at the bottom of Grafton Street it was dark and she was instantly enveloped in the Saturday evening joie de vie of those around her. She joined the throng and made her way to the restaurant, hoping Kevin had beaten her there and was waiting outside as they'd arranged.

He was! She glimpsed his dark head and lean, rangy form beneath the neon glow as he stood waiting out the front of the restaurant. She weaved her way in and out of the moving foot traffic and as she drew closer, she saw he had his hands shoved in the pockets of his leather jacket. She liked that jacket, it gave him a roguish quality. He'd been wearing it when he'd come to the guesthouse to fix the broken lock on Room 6's door. Bronagh thought it most fortuitous, as the handsome fella arrived with his toolbox in tow, that her finger had stopped on Under Lock & Key in the telephone book when she'd been searching for a local locksmith to call.

When he'd finished the job, he'd paused to chat and she'd discovered he was from Donegal originally. She'd holidayed there once when she was younger and her dad was alive, Mam still well, and Hilary not so full of delusions of grandeur. He knew the bay where they'd rented their holiday cottage well and their conversation had been easy as it flowed from there.

She'd made him a cup of tea, hoping Maureen wouldn't come down the stairs and find her chatting up a tradesman, plying him with tea and biscuits. She didn't feel too guilty because he was being paid for the job not by the hour, unlike herself! Before he'd left, he'd asked her if she'd like to meet him on Saturday night for a meal, suggesting Captain America's for the craic. Bronagh had said yes and spent the rest of the week counting down the hours until Saturday.

Now, it was finally here and she saw, instead of the jeans and old plaid shirt he'd been wearing under his jacket when he'd come to the guesthouse, he'd scrubbed up well. He was dressed in a black skivvy with a pair of tight camel trousers and she watched two girls nudge one another as they walked past eyeing him up. Oh yes, he was a heartthrob alright, and he was also oblivious to the female attention. She wanted to pinch herself at the realisation it was her, Bronagh Hanrahan, he was waiting for.

'Hello,' she said, suddenly shy now she was here, as she stepped into his line of sight.

'Bronagh! You look great.' He leaned in and kissed her on the cheek. She inhaled the leather of his jacket and clean-shaven soapy smell of his skin and a thrill coursed through her.

'Thank you.'

'Are you hungry?'

'Starving!' She laughed as he held the door open for her and the music and smell of frying chips washed over her.

Present

Bronagh blinked, finding herself back in the kitchen as Linda's bawdy chuckle sounded from the front room and the memories from the past began to fade. Not before she remembered what a gas the night she'd had with Kevin had been on that long-ago evening. He'd had her laughing over her shoe-string fries at the stories he'd told her about some of the situations he'd inadvertently found himself called out to. And, who'd have thought the man quietly strumming the guitar and singing in the corner of the restaurant, a glass of wine at his side, would go on to have all those hit songs. She had a Chris de Burgh album somewhere; she must give it a dust off.

She was about to pick up her pen again to finish her letter when she heard her mam call out.

'Bronagh.'

'What is it, Mam?'

'Do you know if we've any glue? We're after running out.'

She sighed; she'd come back to her letter in a moment, and getting up she went to check in the flotsam-jetsam drawer.

Chapter 17

'MAMMY'S BEEN MISSING in action twice this week,' Moira said to Aisling, who was working her way through her last piece of morning toast. They were sitting opposite each other at the dining room table, Moira toying with her bowl of cereal. Quinn was still in bed as he'd had a rowdy table of guests last night at the bistro, who'd stayed until well after closing despite, Paula's non too subtle clearing of the table and Tom's announcement the bar was shut. It was strange getting used to Quinn being around, Moira mused, lifting her spoon and tipping the milk on it back into the bowl.

'Are you going to eat that or play with it?' Aisling said, ignoring her sister's Mammy MIA lament. They both knew where she was after all so she was hardly missing in action.

Moira wasn't listening. She was thinking about how she now had to remember not to dash from bedroom to bathroom in just her knickers. Disturbingly, she'd discovered in the short time since he'd moved in, Quinn was a leaver upper of the toilet seat, something she'd already had to have words with Aisling about. Still and all, she thought, forgetting her cereal and picking up her tea instead, so far as brothers-in-law went, Quinn was a good one, not like the chinless feck, Rosi had been married to. Jaysus wept, she couldn't have shared a home with him. There'd have been murder. No, she loved Quinn and she was happy for him and Ash, it was just there were so many changes happening at the moment and she'd never been very good with change.

Take Aisling for instance. There she was now, a married woman living with her husband in the apartment the two of them had rubbed along in by themselves for the last few years. No longer could she sneak in to Ash's bedroom and help herself to whichever shoes went best with her current choice of outfit because effectively she was now sneaking into Aisling *and* Quinn's bedroom and that put a different spin on things. It didn't feel right. Then there was this business with Mammy stopping out at her man friend's. It was very unsettling her having not been home on Monday night or Wednesday night either.

Aisling got up from the table and Moira registered her plate clattering into the sink before she took herself off to her bedroom.

Tom was making noises about her moving in with him at his flat but she wasn't sure she was ready for that. For one thing she'd have to split the rent with him which wouldn't be easy on her current allowance. For another, she was fairly certain she'd find his flatmates, two fellow student doctors, Tamar and Malcolm, annoying. All they talked about was medicine and there was only so much you wanted to hear about the human anatomy when you were trying to watch *Fair City* or *Bally K*.

She finished her tea and gave up on the cereal, getting up to clear her things away. She had to be considerate now too. Once upon a time she'd have left her dishes on the worktop and waited for the magic fairy to wave her wand and clean up but she felt badly about Quinn getting up after working hard at the restaurant to find a bombsite in the kitchen. She'd just loaded her bowl in the dishwasher when she heard her sister bellow.

'Moira, did you wear my black Valentino booties while I was away?'

She picked up her art folder and slung her satchel over her shoulder, heading out the door lickety-split.

MAUREEN'S WEEK WAS flying by. Sure, it was a blur of singing lessons, line dancing, watercolour class, yoga pant party promotion, and then there was Donal; she'd seen him twice. He'd stayed at her place on Tuesday night after they'd gone for a meal here in Howth and he'd invited her to his house for the first time for dinner on the Wednesday night, not ready for them to part company. Maureen mused over this as she ran the hoover across the carpet. She and Donal had entered new territory now and she'd found herself in a quandary once she'd accepted his dinner invitation. Did she pack a toothbrush and bring Pooh whom she couldn't leave overnight on his own or was that being presumptuous? She'd stewed on it until she'd decided she was being ridiculous. Honesty and openness, was the key in any relationship and so, she'd rung Donal and come right out with it. He'd said he'd like it very much if she were to bring her toothbrush and Pooh was welcome too, he'd plenty of Kenny CDs to keep him happy.

She'd been pleased to see he was house proud and she'd commented on this but he'd given her a rueful grin and confessed Louise came by once a week and gave the place a going over for him despite his protesting he was perfectly able to do it himself. She was a very capable woman, Donal said. She had all these balls in the air between work, family life and the various boards she sat on but she managed them all. Louise's children, Brody and Katie, grinned down at her from framed photographs on the walls as they flashed missing front teeth, each child sporting an abundance of freckles. The walls were decorated with pictures showcasing family life and she'd been drawn over to see for herself this other side of Donal she'd not yet been privy to.

She'd wondered, without consciously admitting so, whether she resembled his late wife in any way. People had a type after all, but as she looked at the woman dimpling down at her, she could find none. Ida had the type of smile that lit up her entire face and her pronounced dimples made Maureen think she'd have had a good sense of fun. She'd worn her hair in a practical, short style which suited her elfin features and from what Donal had told her would have suited a life that was busy and full. She'd been an active member of the PTA at the school their girls had gone to, had worked part time as a nurse, volunteered for a support line, done Donal's books and managed to squeeze in badminton twice a week. Where Donal was a big man, she was petite to the point of dainty. She thought she'd have probably liked this woman if they'd had the opportunity to meet. She hoped Ida would have approved of her too.

Maureen turned her attention to a portrait of his girls as teenagers. Louise, the elder of the two, took after her father, a big-boned girl with mischievous grey eyes, whereas Anna had the pixie look of her mammy; she'd inherited her dimples too.

Anna, Donal informed her as he checked the vegetables he'd brought to the boil in a pot on the stove, kept his freezer stocked with ready meals she'd make when she had time off, dropping around a week's worth to see him right until her next batch. She did it so he didn't have to think about cooking a meal for one if he'd been working. It had made Maureen feel strange hearing this on top of Louise doing his housework for him. Before she'd had time to work out how she could tactfully inquire as to why he didn't do these things himself she'd blurted out. 'And who cut your legs off then?'

Donal had laughed and told her his girls liked to feel needed. He agreed he was perfectly capable of doing the housework and cooking his meals, the proof of which was in the delicious casserole bubbling in his oven, but they'd fallen into routines since Ida had passed. He didn't want to rock the boat, he'd said. Maureen had pushed the unsettled feeling this information wrought aside. Her girls were beginning to soften where Donal was concerned, she was sure of it. His girls would accept her in their daddy's life, too.

As she skirted around the sofa sucking up curly poodle hairs, a shiver of trepidation passed through her. How would they take their daddy having a new woman in their life? She'd cross that bridge when she came to it. First things, first. There was a yoga party to be organising.

Chapter 18

1971

BRONAGH COULD FEEL the package, wrapped in a masculine brown gift wrap paper, burning a hole in the side pocket of her mini-dress as she flapped out the blanket in order to lay it on the grass. She'd arranged to meet Kevin here at midday. The People's Garden in Phoenix Park was a favourite spot of theirs and she was laying the blanket beside the formal flowerbeds. Behind her the obelisk reared up, separated by the rustling leaves of the line of trees which, if the sun got too hot, they could move under for some shade later.

She bent over, receiving a wolf-whistle for her efforts as she straightened the blanket and hastily sat down. The perpetrator was a spotty jack-the-lad who looked as though he was barely out of school; he was elbowing his pals who were all leering over. She gave them a haughty look before opening the picnic basket so as to have something to do while she waited for Kevin. He was late she realised, but that wasn't a surprise. Timekeeping wasn't his strongest suit. Her mouth watered at the sight of the bacon wrapped spam bites and cheese quiche along with a chocolate cake, Kev's favourite, all made that morning. The Tupperware she'd bought at the party her friend Jeannie had tried to talk her into having a go at selling was wonderful for transporting food, she mused. The bacon bites were calling to her and her tummy rumbled. No, Bronagh, she told herself, wait for Kevin and she shut the lid on temptation.

Mam had commented on how short the skirts were the girls got about in these days as she'd made to leave the house earlier. She'd launched into an 'in my day' commentary as Bronagh picked up the picnic basket, pushing her hair back over her shoulders. 'It's fashionable, Mam,' she'd replied, patting her pocket to check the present was there before casting a glance down at her yellow dress.

She'd bought it last summer and had decided she could get away with airing it for another season. The cotton fabric was decorated with bold orange flowers, had capped sleeves, a white Peter Pan collar and yes, it managed to cover her backside, but only just. Her legs were beginning to get a bit of colour she'd noticed, pleased to see they were a shade of honey instead of the pasty white they'd been when she'd finally been able to tuck away her winter gear.

'And a bird could nest in that hair, Bronagh,' her mam had added for good measure. Bronagh had seen the twinkle in her eye and knew she was teasing.

It was true though, she'd teased and sprayed it within an inch of its life, securing it back from her face with an Alice band. It was the longest she'd ever worn it. Kevin loved her hair; he'd told her it was her crowning glory and she repeated that sentiment to her mam.

'Ah, go on with you and enjoy yourselves. You've a grand day for it. Remember I'm making the dinner.'

Bronagh had kissed her on the cheek. 'I'm looking forward to it and so's Kev, Mam.' Her mam was enjoying a spell of feeling well. The warmer weather helped as she wasn't as susceptible to picking up the bugs that saw her go downhill for such long periods. As such, she was determined to cook a birthday dinner for Kevin whom she was growing as fond of as Bronagh was.

She'd called out a goodbye and closing the door behind her had headed down the street to catch the bus to Phoenix Park. Kev had high hopes of saving enough for a car soon and said they'd go all over the show then. She looked forward to it but for today, Phoenix Park was as good a place as any to enjoy a lazy afternoon in the sun.

Now she stretched her legs out, enjoying the warmth of the sun caressing them. Kevin was turning twenty-seven and she'd found the perfect present for him. She couldn't wait to see his face when he opened it. A bee buzzed past her ear and she sat still as it went on its way. She could hear the distant shouts of children playing and the odd duck quacking. The sounds of summer were all around her and she inhaled the scent of sweet grass as she scanned the faces of the people meandering around the Victorian formal gardens. There was no sign of Kevin though. He was half an hour late now but she couldn't get annoyed with him on his birthday so she busied herself admiring the reds, oranges and pinks of the well-tended flowerbeds.

She brought Mam here sometimes when she was up to an outing. It was such a beautiful place and, Bronagh thought, to just laze and enjoy the splendour of nature was good for the soul. She'd not extended the invitation for her to join them today, even though she'd have enjoyed a jaunt, because she wanted to be on her own with Kev when she gave him his gift. It had a very special message for his eyes only on it.

The last outing they'd taken Mam on was to Greystones. It had been a day like today and the three of them had climbed aboard the Dart, Kevin supporting Mam on one side, her on the other. They'd all enjoyed the scenic train journey along the coast and when they'd gotten off, they'd sat in the beer garden of a pub and admired the blue-green waters rolling in on the pebbly shore. It had been lovely to see the twin spots of pink appear on her mam's cheeks from the fresh salty air. Kevin was so good with her, she often thought. He never complained when he suggested she join them, understanding how, since she'd become ill, people had stopped inviting her out. Bronagh didn't like the thought of her being cooped up at home when she was fit enough to venture out.

She glimpsed his familiar figure strolling lazily through the gardens. Kevin was never in a hurry to get anywhere and Bronagh would tease him if he was any more laid back, he'd fall over. She sat up straight and shielding her eyes from the sun, waved out. He raised his hand back but his pace didn't increase and she waited patiently, beaming up at him as he greeted her before flopping down on the blanket beside her. He leaned over for a kiss, his hair falling into his eyes and she obliged enthusiastically.

'Happy Birthday,' Bronagh breathed as they broke apart, her eyes still half closed.

'And a grand birthday present that kiss was too,' he grinned. 'Sorry I'm late. My mam telephoned to wish me happy birthday as I was about to head out the door and the whole tribe took turns singing it down the phone.'

Bronagh could tell he was pleased to have heard from them; she knew how he much he missed his family. 'Mam says happy birthday too and she's busy cooking up a storm at home.' An exaggeration, but she was pleased to see Kevin's face shine at the thought. He deserved a lovely day, she thought, unable to wait any longer. She reached inside the pocket of her skirt and produced the package. 'This is for you.'

'You didn't have to do this.' He grinned, but ripped it open in a manner that suggested he was pleased she had. He looked at the box for a moment before opening it and pulling out the solid silver Zippo lighter contained inside. It gleamed in the sun and he admired the weight of it as he held it in the palm of his hand. 'Bronagh, it's great.' His face said it all and she felt a lovely popping like champagne bubbles inside her as he gazed at the side embossed with a Celtic cross. She held her breath waiting for him to turn it over and see what she'd had inscribed on the other side. He did so, reading out loud, 'For Kevin, Love Bronagh.' She'd agonised over whether to include the L word; they hadn't said it to one another as such but in the end, she'd decided to be bold because she was in love with Kevin and she wanted him to know it.

He'd pushed his hair out of his eyes and looked at her as the sun beat down and said, 'This is the best present I've ever been given. I love it and I love you, Bronagh Hanrahan.'

Chapter 19

ROSI PUSHED THE TROLLEY upon which she had two large suitcases stuffed full of yoga pants in small, medium and mostly large. She'd been worried she might get stopped leaving London when her cases had gone through the X-ray machine and the officer in charge had beckoned her aside, asking to see inside them. She'd found herself gabbling her explanation, as she always did when confronted with figures of authority, as to why she had so many pairs of soft, stretchy pants in her possession. She couldn't get done for smuggling, could she? It wasn't illegal to carry one hundred pairs of yoga pants into another country was it? Apparently not, because by the time she'd finished the officer was shaking his head trying to understand the relevance of Tupperware and yoga pants as he waved her on through.

Noah and Mr Nibbles were at his grandmother and father's this weekend. She'd arranged for Colin to pick their son and his gerbil, who'd had a class visit for the day, directly from the school's gates as she was leaving work a couple of hours early to get her flight. She was fortunate his teacher had allowed Mr Nibbles back in her classroom after the show and tell debacle where he'd escaped and terrorised the principal in the toilets. She was kind-hearted, Noah's teacher, and Roisin suspected none too fond of the stern head. It was still odd this business of weekend sharing her son with Colin and she doubted she'd ever get used to Noah not being with her all the time but he needed his dad and as for his Granny Quealey, well she was a pain in the arse but she did love him. Surely, the more people in the world who loved your child the better.

Noah normally would've had a tantrum of planet-exploding proportions at the notion of missing out on a trip to Dublin to see his beloved aunts and nana but once she'd explained about the party, he'd been happy to take a rain check. It wasn't a party at all, he'd stated because there wasn't going to be little red sausages, cake and pop. Roisin had been glad insomuch as she'd envisaged scenarios whereby Mr Nibbles had gotten loose. It wouldn't be the first time the gerbil had tasted freedom. Oh no, she couldn't risk having him terrorising the poor women who'd decided to come to the party, hopefully for a gander at the yoga pants and not just the free glass of wine.

Of course, the weekend wasn't going to be all about yoga pants and meeting Mammy's man friend, Donal and his family was going to be interesting and she'd be getting in Moira's ear about behaving herself. She wondered not for the first time what he'd be like. She pictured a lean, weather-beaten, yachtie type. What would his daughters make of Mammy and of her and her sisters? Yes indeed, it was going to be interesting but the weekend was about Shay, too. She planned on spending as much time as she could with him without getting told off by Mammy, who was after all paying her fare. She wondered how Mammy would take the news she'd organised to stay at his place so as to squeeze every possible moment, in between her family obligations, as she could with him. This business of him being in Dublin and her in London was hard work but it was the way it had to be at the moment. Who knew where they'd be in six months' time? They'd have to see how it went.

The doors to the Arrivals hall opened and she scanned the area. Mammy had told her she would be wearing her yellow airport sweater for visibility purposes. It only took a second before she spied her and began wheeling her trolley toward the woman in a yellow sweater and yoga pants performing lunges for a cluster of women and one man who looked utterly bewildered as to what was going on. For Roisin's part, she was slightly miffed that Mammy wasn't scanning the floor for her oldest daughter and leaping up with excitement at the sight of her. She drew alongside the spectacle and waited for Mammy to stop the side bends she'd moved into and notice her.

Maureen received a smattering of applause when she straightened and spied Roisin. 'Ah grand, here she is, my supplier.'

Roisin glanced around half expecting a customs man to march on over and haul her off to the room where they took the drug mules.

'This is my daughter, everyone, Roisin. She's after bringing the yoga pants in for me. They'll be for sale at a heavily discounted price on Saturday evening at the Howth church hall.'

'Hello there, Roisin,' several accents chimed as they looked her way.

Roisin attempted a smile and nod but they'd already turned their attention back to Mammy who was handing out fliers and telling her audience to remember there'd be wine and finger food on offer too. Sweet Jaysus, Roisin thought, what had she gotten herself into? She waited for the small crowd to disperse.

Once they had, Mammy turned on her heel, still in business mode as she said, 'C'mon, Rosi, we can't be hanging around here all day. We've a party to be getting ready for.'

'What was all that about?' Roisin hissed once out of earshot. 'Making a holy show of yourself with the lunges and the like.'

'It's called sales and networking, Rosi, that's what that was all about, thank you very much.' Maureen shook her head as if it were self-explanatory.

'Yes, but half of those women were foreign.'

'Roisin O'Mara! I didn't raise you to hear talk like that. Sure, they're as entitled as any God- fearing Irish woman to have access to comfortable trousers.'

'I didn't mean it like that.' She'd only been in Dublin ten minutes and she was already exhausted; it was going to be a long weekend. 'I meant they're not going to be wanting to be spending their holidays attending a yoga pants party in Howth, now are they?'

Maureen was beginning to regret her choice of business partner. Rosi never had been the sharpest tool in the shed. 'Roisin.' The tone was pained. 'If you were setting off on your travels around a foreign country and knew you were going to be sitting on your arse on buses for hours on end or in a hire car or whatever else, you'd want to be wearing comfortable trousers while you were doing so, now wouldn't you?'

'I expect so.'

'Well I know so. They'll come, they'll buy, and they'll spread the word, and that my girl is what is called networking and marketing on a global scale. The yoga pant, Tupperware party formula could become a global phenomenon.' Maureen nearly walked into the sliding doors which hadn't opened as fast as they should have as she pictured women around the world holding bonfires as they burned their tight trousers in a symbolic celebration of comfy pants.

'Mammy, would you look where you're going.'

Outside it was already dark, and cold to boot. Roisin shivered despite her thick coat. 'I'm not sitting in the back,' she said as the car was unlocked and she spied his Royal Highness, Pooh the poodle perched in the passenger seat, his eyes gleaming in the darkness challenging her to take him on because he was top dog around here.

'Roisin, you'll do as you're told, now in the back with you.' Maureen clambered behind the wheel.

'It's not right,' Roisin muttered, getting in the back and belting in. It smelt very doggy in here she thought, folding her arms across her chest.

'Zip it, I need to concentrate.'

Roisin ignored her. If she could sit next to a panting poodle then she could manage a grilling about her man friend. 'So, Mammy, we're to have lunch with your Donal fella and his family on Sunday I hear.'

'Say your piece, Rosi, your sisters both have.'

There was no point giving her a hard time; like she'd told Moira they needed to accept Mammy's new friendship and besides she was curious. 'What's he like?'

Maureen's eyes flicked from the rear-view mirror back to the road in front of her again. 'He's a widower with two grown daughters who dote on him by all accounts. Do you know they cook for him and do his housework? What a grand pair of girls they must be.'

'You're perfectly capable of doing your own cooking and cleaning, Mammy,' Rosi retorted. 'We've no desire to take away your independence. What did he do? Assuming he's retired.'

'Semi-retired and he's an electrician. He owns his own home in case you were wondering whether it's my money he's after.'

'No, Mammy, we've Patrick for that.' It slipped out.

Maureen glanced in the rear-view mirror once more but it was too dark for her to make out Rosi's expression. She glossed over the remark, not wanting to get into it with her daughter tonight. 'And he's kind, he makes me laugh and treats me very well. So, there you have it.'

'I should think so.'

'Think so, what?'

'That he treats you well, of course.'

Maureen smiled at Rosi's indignant tone.

'Any man who didn't would have me, Ash, Moira and Patrick to answer to.'

'You sounded like me then, fierce.'

'Well I get it from somewhere,' Rosi said.

'Thank you for not jumping down my throat about him like the other two,' Maureen said.

Rosi enjoyed the mammy, daughter solidarity for a moment and then said, 'Well, Mammy, I know all about second chances and you've every right to one too. Speaking of which I'm going to stay at Shay's tonight and tomorrow.' Her hand shot out and grabbed the front seat headrest as Mammy braked with more force than was necessary at the first set of red lights.

'You've no time for shenanigans when we've a party to be getting organised for. Sure, I'll not be carrying on with Donal either. It's the price a fledgling business has to pay.'

Jaysus wept, her mammy didn't need to be so graphic. Just because they'd had a moment of being on the same page when it came to men didn't mean she had to take it a step further. She was with Moira, it wasn't right!

Chapter 20

ROISIN AND MAUREEN hauled the suitcases across the deserted car park beneath the apartment building Maureen called home and waited for the lift to take them to her level. Pooh was panting at their side. The door slid open and they shuffled inside, Roisin hoping it wouldn't jam between floors on account of their being over the weight limit. She couldn't imagine being stuck in an elevator with her mammy and a poodle for hours on end. It was the stuff of horror films. 'If these don't sell, Mammy, you'll be reimbursing me, you know,' she said as the lift groaned and creaked its ascent.

'Have a little faith, Rosi,' Maureen muttered as she put the case she was holding down.

'How many have you got coming?'

'Around thirty-five or so. Mostly women from my line dancing classes, a handful from golf and watercolour class. The bowls ladies weren't interested because the pants don't come in white and then of course our foreign friends from the airport are likely bets. I put a sign up at the local library too so we may get a few extras.'

The doors pinged open and they dragged the cases on their final leg to Maureen's door where there was a momentary panic she'd lost her house keys. She patted down her pockets locating them in the inside pocket of her coat and finally, they were in.

'We're conference calling your sisters in twenty minutes,' Maureen announced, gesturing for Roisin to leave the case alongside where she'd left the other, over by the wall so as they wouldn't trip over them. She shrugged out of her coat and went to hang it up.

Roisin could detect the familiar scent of Arpège on the air and it made a pleasant change from the poodle smell of the car. She gave the place the once-over looking for evidence of Donal, the man friend as she thought of him, having made himself at home. There were no men's shoes tucked away on the floor beside the sofa, no discarded jumpers, nothing she could see but, and she shuddered, she hadn't checked Mammy's bedroom yet. At least out here though everything was as it had been the last time she'd been over. She saw the wood carved canoe was still in pride of place and shook her head. How her mammy could not see it looked like an ethnic fertility symbol or to put it plainly, *a willy,* was beyond her. She discarded her coat, rolling her eyes at the thought of the impending phone call. Moira and Aisling's idea of a conference call would be the pair of them leaning into the phone talking over top of one another as Mammy overrode them both.

'Don't leave your coat there, you know where to hang it up,' Maureen said, reappearing in time to see Roisin tossing it over the back of the sofa. She went and did as she was told before leaning against the worktop to watch as her mammy bustled about the kitchen. While she warmed the dinner she'd put in the microwave for Roisin, Rosi took a moment to observe her. She'd lost weight; the yoga pants had been fit to burst, indecently so the last time she'd seen her. Now, she didn't feel like screaming, 'Watch out, Mammy, you'll have the arse out of those,' each time she bent over. There was a glow about her too and a lightness to her step. She knew exactly what it was because people had pass-remarked to her how well she was look-ing since she'd met Shay. They'd even done so when her fringe had been halfway up her forehead after being butchered by her so-called hairdresser friend. It was called being in love. She couldn't begrudge her mam those happy, warm feelings, she de-cided but she could begrudge her not letting her go and see the man she'd fallen in love while she was in Dublin.

She pulled her mobile phone out and moved over into the living room area before telephoning Shay to let him know she'd arrived and was at her mammy's. She felt sixteen years old again as she hatched a plan for him to pick her up at ten o'clock that evening, only this time she wouldn't be creeping down the stairs when her mammy and dad thought she was tucked up in bed before roaring off on the back of a motorbike! The sound of Shay's voice, and knowing he was near, perked her up and she even managed to give Pooh a fuss once she'd gotten off the phone.

'Don't think I didn't hear you plotting,' Maureen said as the microwave pinged.

'Ah, Mammy, I hardly get to see him as it is and sure by the time, he picks me up, we will have sorted this party of yours out and you'll be wanting to go to bed.'

'Our party, Rosi, and fair play to you but you'd better not disappear tomorrow. I want you back here at the crack of dawn.'

'I won't. I promise.' Nine o'clock was plenty early enough, she decided.

'Make yourself useful and close the curtains would you. I should have done it before I went to pick you up.'

Roisin obliged but as she went to shut the blinds overlooking the balcony, she let out a shriek. 'Mammy there's a giant rat on your outdoor furniture. It's got glowing eyes and it's staring at me as if it wants to eat me!'

'Jaysus wept, Roisin. Aisling's the drama queen not you.' Maureen moved to where Rosi was shuddering at the spectacle outside. 'It's Peaches, you eejit, the Persian next door is all.'

Roisin leaned in close to the window for a better look, her breath leaving a misty patch. 'It's got a pom-pom on the end of its tail and around its feet. That's not normal.'

'That's down to her next door, she's after entering the cat in a competition and she's aiming for Peaches to take out the title of Supreme Cat.' Maureen was taking a plate out of the microwave.

'It frightened me so it did, Mammy.' Roisin held her hand to her chest. 'My heart's still banging away.' She closed the blinds, not wanting those beady eyes watching her eat her dinner.

Maureen carried the plate over to the table.

'Is it your homemade pie, Mammy?' Rosi asked, sitting down in front of the steaming pile of creamy mashed potato and beef mince with baby beans. She was hoping a glass of wine might be offered because she could do with one after the encounter she'd just had. She was in luck, she thought, seeing Mammy open a bottle of red.

'It is, Rosi.' She knew the pie was her daughter's favourite.

Roisin began to tuck in, her earlier horror at her mammy talking about carrying on and the likes forgotten, almost. If she was still making cottage pie for her with lashings of creamy mashed spud on top, then she was still Mammy. 'Are you going to pour that or are we just going to admire the bottle?' She gestured to the wine bottle standing open on the table.

'I'm letting it breathe, Roisin. Good things take time.'

'It'll be time for me to go home by the time you get around to giving me a drink.' Rosi picked up her glass and held it out.

Maureen sighed, saying something about heathen children as she poured Rosi's glass. She helped herself too because if you couldn't beat them you might as well join them.

Rosi cleaned up her plate in no time and washed it up before settling herself on the sofa. Maureen busied herself finding the notepad on which she'd written out a list delegating various tasks between her, Rosi, Aisling and Moira. She checked to see Pooh was happy in his basket and wouldn't be interrupting their call before glancing at the time. 'Right, it's time to phone the girls.' She sat down next to Rosi so she could lean in and follow the conversation, hearing it ring a couple of times before it was answered.

'Aisling? It's your mammy.' Maureen took charge before Roisin could open her mouth to speak.

'I know who it is, Mammy. You said you were going to be calling at this time.'

'Is your sister there?'

'I'm here, Mammy,' Moira chimed in before asking, 'Is Rosi there?'

'I'm here.'

'How're you, Rosi? Good flight was it?' Moira asked.

'Grand. A little bumpy ten minutes in mind.'

'Aisling, Moira, there'll be plenty of time for chit-chat with your sister later. This is a business call and as such I'll do the Minutes. I'm after ticking off you're all present.'

Roisin watched as her mammy did just that.

'Moira, Aisling, have you a notepad and a pen ready like I asked you?'

'Yes, Mammy,' Aisling replied.

'Good, let's begin. Moira, you're going to be our waitress for the evening and I want you to write this down. You're NOT to go your own way and wear anything that shows your knickers because you'll put the ladies off their finger food. I want us all in the yoga pants so as to demonstrate their versatility. Did you write that down?'

'We must all be wearing the yoga pants,' Moira repeated. 'To show everybody you can hand out drinks and finger food while wearing them without flashing your knickers.'

Maureen frowned. It was always hard to tell whether Moira was being smart or not. She moved on to Aisling. 'I've you down for working the room, Aisling. You're going to be our glamour girl.'

'Mammy, that's not fair,' Moira butted in. 'She's an old married woman. I should be the glamour girl.'

'No, Moira, you always look bandy legged to me when you wear the high heels. We want to *sell* the yoga pants not put people off. Aisling has the knack of walking properly in them and a glamour girl has to wear high heels.'

Roisin snorted which didn't escape Moira. 'I don't know what you're laughing at John Wayne.'

'What's that supposed to mean?' Roisin frowned.

'If anybody's getting about the place walking all bandy legged like a cowboy it's you after you've been visiting Shay and doing the r—.'

'God Almighty, I'll bang yer heads together, so I will,' Maureen huffed.

Roisin bit back her retort, given she was in her mammy's close vicinity and would not be able to duck a cuff around the ear.

Maureen waited a beat, satisfied nobody else would be piping up with any smart-arse remarks. 'As I said, Aisling, is the glamour girl and I'll hear no more about it, Moira. Rosi, do you think Aisling will fit the yoga pants, she's after eating a lot on her holidays?'

'It was a honeymoon, Mammy and I didn't eat that much.' Aisling was indignant.

'There's plenty of stretch in them, Mammy,' Roisin answered, as her and Maureen shared a conspiratorial look, both knowing Aisling was prone to stuffing her face in cold weather. It was a natural defence to it for her.

'Rosi's our demonstrator,' Maureen said, giving the nod to her daughter.

'On how to walk like a cowboy,' Moira couldn't resist adding.

'Enough!' Maureen thundered. 'Rosi will be showing our ladies how you can do the bendy yoga in the pants.'

All three sisters rolled their eyes; they were yoga pants after all.

'And what will you be doing, Mammy?' Aisling asked.

Maureen took a big breath and puffed up self-importantly. 'I, Aisling will be taking down orders, networking and, depending how we go for time, line dancing. Rosi will come food shopping with me in the morning. I've a list of what we need, and I expect you two here by four o'clock at the latest to help me make the hors d'oeuvres. Are we all clear?'

'Ten-four, over and out, Mammy,' Moira said.

'Clear, Mammy,' Aisling said.

Roisin nodded.

'Alright then, early nights all round tonight. I want you all in top form tomorrow.'

'Tell that to Rosi, Mammy,' Moira leapt in.

'Shut up, Moira! She always has to have the last word, Mammy'

'Don't shout in my ear, Roisin,' Mammy said. 'I'm having the last word because I'm hanging up now.'

Chapter 21

'ROISIN O'MARA, I SAID crack of dawn not ten thirty. Sure, it's nearly lunchtime and you needn't think you're coming in. We haven't got time for cups of tea and cosy chats.' Maureen stepped outside into the corridor and was about to close the door when Pooh shot through, looking as eager for the off as she was. 'No, you're not coming. I've the Kenny Rogers playing for you, off you go. Your favourite song's on after this one. He likes *Daytime Friends* best,' she told Roisin, herding the poodle back in through the door. 'He takes himself off to see if Peaches is on the balcony and gazes out at her while the song plays.'

'Are you saying he's got a crush on the pom-pom Persian next door?' Roisin frowned and she rubbed her temples; her head was already beginning to throb at the thought of the day and evening lying ahead.

'He's confused as to what he is, or that's what I think at least. The vet doesn't agree but sure how would he know? He's not Doctor Doolittle. I'm going to have to introduce him to some poodle lady friends. There's a good-looking girl at the obedience class I take him to but we're always leaving as they're arriving.'

'Star-crossed lovers,' Roisin muttered and then a thought occurred to her. 'But he's been seen to. He's not interested in that sorta thing anymore.'

'Roisin, get your mind out of the gutter. Men and women can be friends you know. We're all partial to a bit of company with the opposite sex now and again. And what's that on your chin?'

Roisin's hand went to where her mammy was peering to feel the tender skin there, already knowing the redness her eagle eyes had spotted was from Shay's in-between beard. He'd stopped shaving a couple of weeks ago and wanted her opinion as to his new look. She liked it but not the rash it had given her. 'I don't know, Mammy, maybe I've an allergy to something?' She shrugged.

'Allergy my arse. I wasn't born yesterday, now come on with you.' She marched her daughter over to the lifts. 'I'm glad to see you're wearing the pants. It's free advertising so it is.'

Rosi glanced down at her yoga pants and at her mammy's. They were like the fecking Bobbsey twins only Mammy's bottom was definitely bigger than hers. She was beginning to rue the day she'd ever worn the fecking things around her.

They got in the lift and pushed the button to take them down to the apartment's underground car park. 'You're not going to go mad with the food and drink are you, Mammy? Because we're wanting to be making a profit. I don't want to go back to London empty handed or out of pocket. I'm planning on putting the money we make toward my yoga studio fund. We can still have this evening nice on a shoestring.'

Maureen donned her pained expression. 'Was I, or was I not the proprietor of a highly respected guesthouse, Roisin?'

'You were but Daddy did the books.'

Maureen made a pooh-poohing noise. 'We were a team, Rosi.'

The weather as the car nosed out of the car park and out on to the main street was good, with scudding white clouds chasing the pale blue sky. Roisin stared out the window watching the world go by. The seaside hub of Howth was alive with Saturday morning visitors and locals alike, all after a sniff of the sea air she saw as they headed away from it toward the supermarket in Sutton Cross.

Once there, a drama ensued over who had a pound to put in the trolley with Roisin insisting they wouldn't need much and sure, they could manage with a basket. Maureen was having none of it and she stopped a passer-by and asked if they could change a fiver for her.

Roisin trailed behind her mammy, who was pushing the trolley like a mammy on a mission, with a sinking heart. She watched as she picked up smelly cheeses, crackers, salamis, olives, sundried tomato and the best bacon, all of which she happily tossed in the trolley. She chewed the ear off the young lad working on the deli counter by telling him all about the antipasto skewers and bacon wrapped water chestnuts along with feta cheese stuffed, bell peppers she and Rosi were going to be busy making that afternoon.

If it was up to Roisin, she'd be putting a couple of bowls of crisps and peanuts about the place and softening their guests up with the cheapest cask wine from the off licence. Sure, she'd seen a few empty bottles of good red wine waiting to go out with Mammy's rubbish. Why couldn't they pour the vinegar casky stuff into those and save themselves a packet, no one would be any wiser? She envisaged her mammy's line dancing ladies all smacking their lips over the delicious wine Maureen was after serving and it made her smile.

It was a good idea, she thought, warming to it the more she turned it over in her mind. She decided there was no harm in running it by Mammy.

'Roisin O'Mara you could peel an orange in your pocket you could,' Maureen replied upon hearing it. However, she gave Rosi a 'we're partners in crime' wink as, with their matching yoga pant bottoms, they made their way down the wine aisle and she picked up enough casks of cheap red, plonk to have the Irish hurling team singing *Danny Boy* and doing a jig.

Chapter 22

BRONAGH HAD NOT LONG got back from posting this week's letter to Leonard. She'd written to tell him she hadn't been quite so enamoured by the Genoise cake she'd partaken of last night. That wasn't to say it hadn't been very nice, because it was, but it had lacked that something extra the carrot cake had had. Probably the cream cheese icing she'd surmised in her letter. Now, she was busying herself trying to find the Marks & Spencer's frozen chicken pasta dinner for two in the freezer. She knew it was in there somewhere because she'd put it away for nights like this when she didn't feel like cooking. She was fidgety and wanted a quick tea, not wanting to bother with thinking about what she and her mam could have to eat. A quick tea was in order and then she'd be off to the party in Howth. She was looking forward to this evening. There was a good film on the tele tonight so Mam would be alright and Hilary usually rang for a chat, too.

There it was, she thought, victorious as she pulled the chicken meal from the freezer and put it on the bench. She switched the oven on to preheat as per the instructions, preferring to do it in the oven, as she liked the way the cheesy sauce crisped around the edges when it was baked. The microwave left it soggy and lacklustre she always thought. As she waited for it to heat, her mind flitted to Hilary.

It had been ages since Mam had been down to Tramore and Hilary hardly ever ventured back to Dublin, proclaiming it a dirty, overcrowded city, full of foreigners these days. It would have been nice for their mam to see more of the grandchildren, too. Children was a loose term these days. Declan and Erin both towered over their little nan and were pushing thirty. They'd both stayed on in Tramore with Erin engaged to a fellow who worked for her dad's solicitor's firm. She worked as a real estate agent while Declan had a good job in the AIB Bank. He enjoyed playing the lad and was showing no signs of settling down. Whenever Bronagh had broached the subject of one or both them coming to see their nan for a weekend, Hilary would tut and say they led busy lives and sure, where would they sleep. Hilary managed to say this in such a way she made Bronagh feel as if she did nothing but sit around on her arse all day and was not at all inclined to offer to give up her bedroom for one of her sister's offspring.

It was a shame both her niece and nephew had been tarred by their mother's brush. Still, she could hardly have expected them to turn out differently. You were a product of your upbringing. Bronagh backtracked on that particular thought because she'd had the same upbringing as Hilary and they were polar opposites. The thought of Erin and Declan not being bothered to pick up the phone to see how their nan was getting on from time to time rankled. All the times her mam had sent money for their birthdays or as a treat to go and do something nice with, not once had they called or written a note to say thank you. How she'd have loved to have heard what the money she could ill afford had been used for. It would have brightened her day no end to hear tales of a new dress or an outing to see a film. This was ignorant behaviour in Bronagh's opinion and if they'd been her children, she'd have stood over them and made them telephone their nan. She'd learned long ago not to put voice to these opinions because it only upset her mam, and sure, what was the point in that? Besides, Mam simply said she didn't send it wanting anything in return from them. She wanted them to know she was thinking about them was all.

Bronagh frowned as she remembered an occasion when Mam had decided, once the children began working, perhaps it was time to stop sending them spends and so she'd posted Erin's birthday card with nothing inside but good wishes. Hilary had rung the moment it had arrived with her nose out of joint because Erin had been most disappointed when she opened her card to find the usual ten pounds wasn't there. Bronagh had wanted to throttle her sister and had thought it a jolly good thing she lived in Tramore because there'd have been murder if she was close by. Mam had been beside herself.

Family was family though, you couldn't pick them, she mused, not for the first time as she removed the cardboard packaging and punched a couple of holes in the seal of the container before sliding it into the warming oven. The birthday card incident wasn't the worst thing Hilary had ever done, Bronagh thought, closing the oven door.

1971

Summer was drawing to a close and Bronagh had been stepping out with Kevin for months now. She was a different woman to the one who'd caught his eye when he'd come to fix the broken door lock at O'Mara's insomuch as she brimmed with the confidence being part of a pair brought with it. Although some would say hers and Kevin's relationship was more of a triangle, Bronagh was oblivious. Others, more kindly inclined, had noticed and commented as to how well she was looking. It wasn't only in the physical sense because she laughed more, the sort of laughter where you threw back your head and laughed until your stomach hurt. Kevin had brought rainbow hues into a life that had been a little beige and she loved him, he loved her too, and Myrna loved him as she would a son.

Bronagh and Kevin had settled into an easy pattern over the last months with him being understanding over their time needing to be shared with her mam. He treated her mam like a queen and she loved him all the more for it. He never complained either that she wouldn't stay overnight at the flat, rising from the bed with the springs that dug into her back and leaving his bedsit to go home each and every time.

On Wednesdays he came for dinner straight from whatever job he'd been on and then he and Bronagh would traipse off for a drink at the local pub, The Four Horses—one of the few that didn't have a problem with a woman frequenting it. Ireland was backward in so many respects she'd think on occasion, but it was home. She'd sip her Babycham and Kevin his pint while they held hands under the table, listening to the live music played on a Wednesday. Friday nights they stayed in with Kevin happy to pass around the bag of sweets he brought to share as they sat watching *The Late Late Show*. Myrna thought the sun rose and set with Kevin.

It was only fair, given they'd been together a while now and had reached a stage in their relationship where it was hard to remember what things had been like before they'd met, Kevin should want her to meet his family. They'd heard all about her and his mam was insistent they come up for a weekend. The family wanted to meet this girl who'd turned their Kev's head. Weekends away were not something Bronagh had entertained since her mam got sick because she didn't like the thought of her home on her own. When she was well she worried she'd be lonely and when she was ill she worried about her toppling over if she were to have one of her dizzy spells. The thought of her hitting her head as she fell, or lying on the ground unable to get up was unbearable. She couldn't very well ask if she could invite her mam to Donegal either. Sure, what sort of impression would that make? She imagined Kevin greeting his mam with, 'This is Bronagh, oh, and her mam, Myrna's come too to see what the craic's like.'

So, when he'd first broached the subject of two nights away with her, she'd skirted around the subject of a weekend in Donegal, giving him a vague, sometime soon, reply. The second time he'd brought it up they'd been lying in his bed in a tangle of sheets with Bronagh desperately trying to ignore the spring poking in her side because she didn't want to move and break the spell around them. As he asked her if she'd give him a date for when they could go because his mam was hounding him, she'd known it wasn't fair not to give him a definitive answer. He was always so considerate of her and mam's situation.

She'd kissed him and told him she'd sort something out for her mam and they'd put plans in place. They'd organised to head up to Donegal in three weeks which gave his mam plenty of notice to have her cottage gleaming and Bronagh time to organise for her mam to have a break in Tramore. It was high time Hilary had her to stay.

The next evening she'd waited until Mam had gone to bed to call her sister. She didn't want her to overhear her conversation and feel as if Bronagh was trying to fob her off.

'Hilary, how're things?' she asked as the phone was answered on the fourth ring.

'Bronagh, this is late for you to be calling.'

'Were you in bed?'

'No, but we've had our supper.'

Bronagh rolled her eyes. Hilary and George were supper people. Every evening, once Declan and Erin were in bed, she'd make a plate of sandwiches and pour them both a gin and tonic. She thought it made them terribly sophisticated. Bronagh hoped they got indigestion from their corned beef sandwiches or whatever they were after eating.

'Is Mam alright?' Hilary inquired.

'She's alright, yes. How're you all?'

'Busy,' Hilary sighed, 'Life's busy. The children have me run off my feet. Are you still with that locksmith chap from Donnybrook?'

Bronagh's hackles rose. 'Kevin's his name and he's from Donegal not Donnybrook.' She managed to keep her tone neutral, determined not to bite. She had to keep Hilary on side while she broached the subject of their mam coming to stay with her for a weekend. 'Yes, I am. Actually, that's why I'm ringing, Hilary. He's asked me to go up north with him for a weekend to meet his family but of course I won't leave Mam on her own.'

'No, of course you wouldn't,' Hilary snipped, sarcastically.

'What do you mean by that?' Bronagh forgot her resolve of only moments earlier.

'Well, honestly, Bronagh, sometimes I don't know who's more reliant on who. It can't be easy for that fellow of yours always playing the third wheel. Nobody loves a martyr, you know.'

Bronagh was indignant but managed to keep her voice down. 'I'm not and he's not the third wheel! And Kevin thinks the world of Mam for your information. I think you've a bare faced cheek criticising me when you never lift a finger to help.'

'I've my family to be thinking of. They've got to come first. You've let Mam become reliant on you, Bronagh. There were other options for the times she's poorly but you insisted on managing her care on your own.'

'Because she's our Mam and I don't want a stranger looking after her.'

They'd reached an impasse and the ensuing silence was deafening. Bronagh, whose heart was thudding from the altercation, could hear the theme tune of whatever programme Hilary and George were watching being played, despite the television being in the living room and her sister standing in the hall. She decided to come right out with it and say what she'd intended to say at the beginning of their conversation. 'Like I said, Hilary, I don't want a stranger looking after her and Kevin's asked me to go to Donegal with him to meet his family so, how're you fixed to have Mammy come and stay with you for the last weekend of this month? I've looked into it and there's a bus I can see her onto that leaves Dublin at two o'clock on the Friday afternoon.'

'But how would she get to the station, you'd be at work wouldn't you?' Hilary shot back.

'It's all sorted. I've asked Maureen O'Mara my employer if I could leave a few hours early on the Friday and she said it's not a bother.' She could visualise her sister's face working as she tried to find a reason as to why it wouldn't work. She had to come up with something that wouldn't put her in a bad light because Hilary was all about keeping up appearances and being seen to do the right thing. She'd hate for anybody to think she left the care of their mam solely to Bronagh, even if she did seem to think Bronagh had foisted that role on herself. This was why she wasn't going to make it easy for her. She was Mam's daughter too and she could jolly well pull her weight.

'The last weekend in November you say?' Hilary said.

'Yes. It's all arranged.' Bronagh wasn't giving her an inch. 'Kev's family's expecting us and Mammy is due to see you and the children. It would save you all piling up to Dublin for a visit now, wouldn't it?'

Hilary would be choking on her G&T. 'Well, I'd have to check with George of course.'

'Of course. Why don't you ask him now? You said you were still up. It will save you having to phone me back.' She pictured her sister, red-faced, steam coming out her ears.

'Give me a moment.'

Bronagh heard the clatter of the phone being put down on the hall table and then voices at a muffled distance. She shifted from foot to foot waiting for her sister to come back on the line and say whatever she was going to say.

Hilary's tone was clipped when she finally picked up the phone. 'George and I have had a chat and yes, that will be fine.'

'Grand.' She wouldn't say thanks. Myrna was her mam too, why should she? 'I'll talk to her about it in the morning. She'll be excited to have a holiday and to see you and George and the children. I'll let you get back to your supper then. Give my love to George and the children.'

She hung up before Hilary could get a word in, not wanting any more cross words between them and put the phone back in its cradle. She had a bubbling sense of excitement she knew would make it tricky for her to sleep. It was going to happen! She was going to Donegal to meet Kev's family. She'd have to think about what she was going to take to wear because she wanted to make the best impression she could, especially on his mam because she knew he doted on her. She was nervous too, determined they like her because Kevin had been talking about their future lately and she had a feeling a proposal might be on the cards. She already knew she'd say yes if it was forthcoming.

Chapter 23

'HOW MANY MORE OF THESE fecky skewer things do I have to make?' Roisin moaned from where she was stationed at the worktop in the kitchen, threading cheese, olives and fancy thin slivers of ham called prosciutto onto bamboo skewers. She was sick of looking at the things and feeling sick from the number of olives she'd snaffled when Mammy wasn't looking. She was partial to the green fruit and hadn't been able to help herself.

'Until you've used everything we bought for the skewers up. And don't think I haven't noticed you stuffing your face, so,' Maureen batted back from her end of the work station where she was artfully arranging crackers on her cheese board.

Roisin marvelled over her all-seeing ability.

They had an hour until they needed to head down to the church hall to set up for the party. Kenny Rogers was crooning softly in the background. Pooh was curled up in his basket, occasionally venturing out to investigate what they were doing in the hope a piece of meat might come his way—with the price of the prosciutto he was fat out of luck. When nothing was forthcoming, he'd mooch over to the doors leading to the deck to see if Peaches was back; she wasn't and he'd stalk huffily back to the basket and so it went.

A knock at the door interrupted their flow and Maureen washed her hands calling out an 'I'm coming' before going to answer it.'

Moira and Aisling bowled in and Roisin looked up from her task. It was all the excuse she needed to take a break and she ran her hands under the tap, drying them on the apron her mam had supplied her with before giving them both a hello hug.

'Nice pinny,' Moira sniggered, checking out the embroidered wine glass and crown above the words 'Your Wineness' Roisin had on overtop of her sweater and yoga pants. Remembering she was the one who'd bought it for Mammy in the first place, she stopped.

'Rosi's put a pair of yoga pants out for you both in the spare room but before you go and get changed, I've a job for one of you.'

'Moira will do it.' 'Aisling will do it.'

'You'll both do as you're told. Moira, you can hold the bottle, she'll pour,' Maureen pointed to Aisling. 'You've a steadier hand.'

'What are you on about, Mammy?' Aisling asked, following her over to the kitchen.

Maureen directed them to a clear spot on the worktop and retrieved the casks of wine she and Rosi had bought earlier.

'Jaysus wept, Mammy, did you buy up Dublin's supply of cask wine. That stuff's like drinking vinegar so it is.' Aisling grimaced.

'Paint stripper,' Moira added.

Maureen was undeterred as she retrieved the two bottles of red she'd enjoyed on different occasions with Donal.

'What are you up to?' Aisling asked, noticing Roisin grinning.

'It's a cost saving exercise,' Roisin told her sister.

'The cask wine is to be poured into these bottles and when we run out you're to repeat the process but be sure no one sees you doing so.'

'Mammy!' Aisling said. 'You can't do that.'

'Oh yes, I can. No one will know the difference and they'll all be happy thinking they're after getting a free glass or two of top-class wine. It's a win, win.'

'I think it's very devious, Mammy, but smart,' said Moira.

'It was actually my idea,' Roisin said.

'Nice one.'

Aisling looked at her mammy and sisters. It was sneaky and underhand but it was oh, so clever and she and Moira set about their task.

Maureen was wiping down the worktop and Roisin was flopped in an armchair eating a hastily slapped together cheese sandwich as the olives had digested and she was hungry. There was no chance of a proper dinner as she waited for her sisters to finish getting ready so this would have to do. The platters were covered in cling film and ready to be taken to the church hall along with the wine and extra cask supplies to be topped up as and when needed.

'Ta-dah!' Aisling chirruped, stepping into the room. 'Glamour Girl or what?' She twirled Wonder Woman-style, her long red-gold hair splaying out around her.

Rosi snorted at the sight of her. She was wearing a plunging red velvet top that left nothing to the imagination along with yoga pants and strappy Valentino heels.

'You'd be more at home in the Rio Carnival than in a church hall in Howth,' she said. 'Look at the state of yer bosom jiggling all over the place.'

'Aisling, you look grand but Roisin's right, a bra wouldn't go amiss. Go on with yer and put them away,' Maureen stated

Aisling glanced down and saw she was exposing her left nipple. 'Feck,' she said, tucking herself back in her top. She'd have to watch that but she couldn't wear a bra under this top, you'd see the lacy edges and straps.

Moira appeared next, having teemed her yoga pants with a black top and sensible shoes.

'You remind me of Michael Jackson for some reason, you just need a sparkling white glove,' Roisin tittered.

'That's not helpful.' Maureen gave her a cuff around the ear. 'Moira, well done you look smart.'

Moira was enjoying not being the one in trouble for a change and wondered if perhaps she should turn over a new fecky brown-noser leaf. 'Are you going like that, Mammy?' she asked, taking in her mam's bumble bee ensemble. 'I thought you saved that outfit for the airport?'

'Sweet Mother of Divine, I've forgotten all about getting changed and me the hostess! Give me five minutes, girls.'

Aisling and Moira joined their sister in lounging around as they waited for Mammy to get ready. They caught up on each other's news.

'How're you finding living with Aisling and—'

'My husband,' Aisling jumped in.

'She does that all the time, it's really annoying,' Moira said. 'Quinn's great but he leaves the loo seat up and they're always,' she pulled a disgusted face, 'fondling one another.'

'Fondling!' Rosi said, trying not to choke on the remains of her cheese sandwich. 'Where did you get that word from?' It conjured up all sorts of lurid images.

Moira shrugged. 'Well, they are.'

'No, we're not. She's exaggerating. You know what she's like, Rosi. We're very mindful of you and not making you feel uncomfortable, so we are.'

'Well you could have been more mindful last night when the bed springs were squeaking. I was so traumatised I couldn't sleep. I'm thinking about moving in with Tom but I have to work out the logistics.'

'What logistics?' Aisling asked, already imagining cosy breakfast table scenes with her and Quinn, no Moira sitting down the end with a face like that Persian that kept showing up on Mammy's balcony.

'How I'm going to pay my half of the rent.'

Maureen reappeared, halting all further conversation as her daughters took stock of her.

She had her rhinestone blouse on, yoga pants and cowboy boots, that wasn't all though.

'Mammy where did you get the cowboy hat from?'

Maureen peered mysteriously out from under the white Stetson. 'I borrowed it from Laura, my line dancing teacher.'

Mammy always took things a step too far, all three sisters silently thought.

Chapter 24

'TEN MINUTES UNTIL SHOWDOWN girls!' Moira clapped her hands, the sound echoing around the church hall.

'Yee-ha,' Moira replied, fist pumping the air, 'And hoe-down!'

'Don't be cheeky.'

'It's the hat,' Aisling whispered to Roisin. 'It's making Mammy behave even more oddly than normal.'

Roisin had to agree. She put her phone back in her pocket having just sent a saucy message to Shay as to what she had planned for them both once she'd escaped the yoga pants party. Moira's Tom had offered to pick them all up after they'd tidied up as he wasn't rostered on at Quinn's this evening. She wondered if he knew what he was in for if her little sister was to move in with him. Poor sod.

The chairs in the church hall were laid out in a semi-circle as per Maureen's instructions. The lighting was as dim as could be expected when dealing with garish fluorescent tubes that had probably been in place since the sixties. It was giving them all a jaundiced look, Roisin thought, glancing at her sisters. The food and wine was in the kitchen off to the side of the hall waiting to be served and Maureen had organised a stack of plastic cups for the wine, and a pile of serviettes too.

'Now then, girls, it's last minute I know but I've decided we need a brand for our pants. I'm after making an executive decision and they're no longer to be called yoga pants.'

'What are we supposed to call them then?' Aisling was puzzled as she glanced down at the pair Mammy had gifted her with. She was rather taken with them, truth be told, they were very comfortable and surprisingly stylish.

'I think the Mo-pant has a lovely ring to it.'

There was a snort from Roisin who'd been doing a lot of that these last few hours and Moira jumped up and down. 'You're naming them after me, Mammy! My very own fashion brand.' This made up for her not being glamour girl.

'Behave yourself. No, I am not. Mo is short for Maureen, you eejit, because this here,' she waved her arm around, 'well, it was my idea so the Mo-pant it is. Maureen's too long-winded and Moira you can wipe that look off your face because your role is important too. You're going to be our guests' first port of call, greeting them as they arrive and issuing them each with one plastic cup and a serviette.'

'Why not a paper plate?' Moira asked sulkily.

'Because, I'm using this.' Maureen tapped the side of her hat. 'You can't load up a napkin the same as you can a plate. We want to stretch the finger food out.' She frowned, or at least that's what Moira thought she was doing. She couldn't see her expression properly beneath the hat. 'And you want to watch out for Joan Fairbrother. She's known for taking more than her share at the bowls club afternoon tea.' She issued Moira with her description leaving her on the lookout for a woman with chunky thighs in her mid-sixties, more than likely wearing a mini-skirt. 'And be sure to keep the wine flowing, the more relaxed our guests are the more likely they are to buy.'

Roisin, Moira and Aisling glanced at one another, not familiar with this shrewd mammy who wore white Stetsons and poured cheap, casky wine into expensive bottles.

'Mammy?' Moira asked.

'You should be getting your cups and serviettes not standing there mammying me.'

'What are you going to be doing while I'm run off my feet being charming to everyone?'

'I'll be standing alongside you directing guests over to the chairs.'

'And what about Aisling and Rosi? What are they going to be doing?'

Maureen rolled her eyes as if it were obvious. 'Aisling will be milling about the place, giving everybody a good gawp at the glamourous side of living in yoga pants.'

'An eyeful of her boobs more like, and you said they're to be called the Mo-pant,' Moira muttered, while Aisling hastily checked she hadn't had fallen out between leaving the apartment and arriving at the hall.

Maureen carried on, 'As for Rosi, she'll be doing a live yoga demonstration.'

'The whole time?'

'No, sure she'd be far too distracting. Only when I introduce her and tell everybody she's going to show us all some proper bendy moves. We're going to play it by ear but I may do a line dance demonstration too.'

Moira turned to her eldest sister. 'Don't you be doing the downward dog, that was a cheese sandwich you were after having at Mammy's and you know what you're like on cheese.'

'Moira, kitchen, now!' Mammy thundered as a head appeared around the door.

'Coo-ee, only me,' said Rosemary Farrell. She limped forth.

Moira hurried off to get the cups and serviettes having no wish to be cornered by Rosemary. The last time she'd seen her, she'd been stuck listening to her go on about her dodgy hip for ages, to the point where Moira had begun imagining her own hip was aching and she'd limped about the place for the rest of the day.

HALF AN HOUR LATER Moira and Maureen had their routine down pat and were proving to be a formidable double act. Moira greeted their guests and handed them the cup and serviette, after which Maureen would steer them towards a chair with a gracious sweep of her arm. They also had a full house which had seen Roisin and Aisling hastily setting out another row of seats for the last-minute guests arriving. Maureen shot Roisin an 'I told you so' look when two of the tourists she'd demonstrated her lunges to in the Arrivals hall of Dublin Airport took a seat. Moira pinpointed a woman fitting Joan Fairbrother's description and took note of where she was sitting so as to move on quick smart once she'd taken her allocated one skewer from the tray. Bronagh also arrived and decided to settle herself near where Aisling was striking a pose. She stared over at her curiously. 'What are you doing, Aisling?' she asked.

'I'm modelling.' Aisling flicked her hair back over her shoulders, one hand on her hip which was thrust forth, a pout in place.

'I see.' Bronagh didn't see at all. Roisin sat down next to her. 'Mammy's after telling her she's the glamour girl. She's demonstrating how the yo-erm, Mo-pant, can be stylish and sophisticated, to show everyone they're not just for exercise, or lounging about.'

'Wine, Bronagh?' Moira asked before Bronagh could reply to Roisin. She was holding up the bottle to ensure Bronagh could see the label.

'Ooh, lovely, I don't mind if I do.'

Moira made the rounds and smirked upon hearing Rosemary Farrell telling her friend, she enjoyed good wine as it helped ease the ache in her hip and this was a fine drop indeed. Maureen had done them proud. She had to duck out back and replenish her bottle more than once and by the time she'd finished filling everyone's cups, Mammy was standing in the centre of the semi-circle about to begin.

'Good evening, ladies and er, gentlemen.'

All heads swivelled back to where Maureen had directed the latter part of her introduction. Roisin felt an urge to giggle but knew she'd cop it from Mammy later if she did. It was the man from the airport who'd watched Mammy's demonstration and he was looking just as bewildered as he had in the Arrivals hall, only now he was beetroot because forty odd women were all eyeballing him. How'd he snuck in without her noticing?

'Thank you for coming,' Maureen beamed. 'We've a grand evening ahead of us with wine, some lovely finger food, and a live yoga demonstration by my daughter, Roisin.'

This time all eyes settled on Rosi and she gave a small wave.

'My name's Maureen for those of you who don't know me and I'm here tonight to introduce you to the Mo-pant.'

'I can't hear you down the back!' shouted, a woman with a helmet of grey hair, a hearing aid visible in either ear.

'Turn them on,' her friend sitting next to her bellowed tapping her own ear.

Maureen thought, there's always one in the room before continuing, her voice a decibel louder. 'The Mo-pant is the one pant for all occasions. The one size fits all pant. It's the comfiest, most flattering pair of pants you'll ever own. First off though, you've met Roisin now say hello to Moira my youngest daughter who's your waitress tonight.'

'Hello, Moira,' came the dutiful reply.

'Could I have a drop more wine, Moira, please, it's going down ever so well, so it is,' said a sweet-faced little lady Maureen recognised from bowls on account of the fact she was a known cheater.

Moira smiled beatifically. 'Certainly.'

'And to my middle daughter, Aisling,' she turned to gesture over to where she'd last seen Aisling who was taking her role very seriously and had decided to improvise. She was strutting around the semi-circle of seating as though stalking the catwalk. Her hand was on her hip and each foot placed carefully in front of the other before she came to a halt beside Maureen turning slowly around affording everyone the chance to check out the Mo-pant from every angle. Unfortunately, her exertions had freed the boob and Maureen hissed in her ear to put it back where it belonged because this was a Mo-pants party, not a peep show.

Roisin felt a dangerous bubble of laughter rise in her throat as she overheard a woman behind her say, 'I don't know if her booby was supposed to be bobbing about like so but sure, her bottom looks grand in the pants.'

'It does, Dolly,' came the reply, 'It reminds me of the story by yer man Dahl. You know the giant peach one.'

'Didn't she do well!' Maureen rallied her crowd, determined to ignore the wardrobe malfunction. They duly applauded and Aisling took herself off to the side, flashing a look at Moira that managed to convey, 'I'm bigger than you so don't you dare breathe a word of my boob walk to anyone' without a single word spoken out loud.

'So you can see, ladies and erm, sir, the Mo-pant looks just as at home here in the church hall as it would out for dinner or at a nightclub.'

'Or strip club,' someone mumbled, as murmurings in the crowd about the naked breast having no place in a church hall began, but any dissent was swiftly quelled by Moira beginning to offer about the platter of tasty skewers. She whipped it by Joan Fairbrother who barely managed to get one in her hot little hand let alone two.

'In a moment,' Maureen said. 'I'm going to pass around two pairs of the Mo-pant and you can feel for yourself how soft and luxurious the material is. Ladies,' she leaned in conspiratorially. 'you're never going to want to wear anything else again.' She handed a pair of pants to the two ladies at opposite ends of the first row of chairs and stood back as they were passed along. 'Feel free to ask any questions.'

'She's very good,' Bronagh said to Roisin in between nibbles of her skewer. 'So's this.' She waggled her cup as Moira passed by indicating she'd like a top up. 'She's like a yoga pant guru, your mam.'

'Mo-pant,' Roisin corrected. She was surprised because her mammy was indeed like one of those women from the infomercials on the television. She was a natural and she fancied she could already hear the purses opening behind her.

By the time Maureen had answered all the questions fired at her and Moira was doing the rounds with the last tray of food, the voices in the hall were noticeably louder and laughter rang out here and there. The wine was going down a treat. Maureen almost rubbed her hands together with delight over how the party was panning out. Self-congratulations would have to wait for now though because it was time for Roisin's demonstration. She made the introduction and sat down in the chair Roisin had just vacated, watching as she laid her yoga mat out.

Rosi told her rapt audience what she was going to do and then ran through a simple sun salutation routine, not heeding Moira's warning about downward dog. She ended her display with a headstand that had the crowd gasping.

'I'd like to be able to do that,' said the woman with the helmet hair and hearing aids.

'Not with your bad shoulder, Flo,' said her friend sitting alongside her.

The pants were taking on magical qualities, sure anything was possible when you were wearing the Mo-Pant! This underlying feeling in the room was exacerbated by Maureen deciding to end things on a lively note. She pushed play on the portable stereo she'd borrowed from Moira and, with a clap of her hands and a turn of her toes, launched into the Tush Push, urging those that wanted to join her to come on up and take a turn on the floor. There was a scraping of chairs followed by a veritable stampede as the women and one man formed two rows following Maureen's lead. Roisin, Aisling, Moira and Bronagh watched their mammy lead the crowd in amazement.

'She almost makes me want to line dance,' Aisling said.

'Me too,' agreed Roisin.'

'That's only because you're drinking the casky wine,' said Moira. 'That's your third cup each.'

'I'm going to give it a go,' said Bronagh, getting up and tagging on the end of the back row.

Needless to say, they sold out of the Mo-pant and Tom wound up being the courtesy driver for a hall full of women who'd had a skinful by home time.

Chapter 25

'MAMMY, MY HEAD HURTS and it's your fault for buying the casky wine,' Aisling bleated down the telephone. She was dressed but only just, and sitting on the sofa sipping a milky brew with an extra teaspoon of sugar in it. The television was flashing bright pictures she was staring at but not seeing in front of her. Quinn was snuggled up next to her on the sofa enjoying a lazy morning with his wife having given up on the idea of anything more than a cuddle because, when he'd made hopeful overtures, she'd told him if he wanted to go riding then he'd best get himself off down to a stables and find a new filly. He'd taken that as a no. She should push him off, she thought, knowing she would've normally been downstairs by now checking in on young James who manned the fort of a weekend. She couldn't summon the energy yet though. Moira was making an unnecessary amount of noise sorting her breakfast out in the kitchen.

'Don't blame me, blame your sister. The cask wine was Rosi's bright idea.'

'I can't blame her, she's at Shay's.'

'How many cups were you after having?'

'Five or six.' Her stomach roiled at the thought of it but she'd needed to blank out the boob incident. Quinn had thought it hilarious when Moira told him what happened and she was currently not speaking to either of them. Moira's earlier words to her had been, 'Forced down your throat was it?' when her sister moaned about the state she was in earlier.

Maureen repeated the sentiment. 'Well, you'll get no sympathy from me, Aisling, nobody forced it down your throat. It serves you right, you should know better at your age.'

'Mammy!' Sympathy and tender loving care was what Aisling needed now.

'Don't Mammy me and don't you be thinking you're wheedling your way out of lunch today either. One o'clock, Aisling, at Johnnie Fox's.'

Aisling sighed. She'd go and see Mrs Baicu, a fry-up would sort her out. 'I know, Mammy, and I don't see why Quinn isn't invited. He's my husband you know.'

'Yes, I do know, Aisling, and Laura's husband's not coming so your Quinn's not either. And tell Moira she's not to wear the skirt that shows her knickers.' Maureen knew she kept mentioning this but she also knew her daughter. 'And you, Aisling O'Mara, under no circumstances are to wear the red top you had on last night. When I think of the Holy show, you with your boob out for all to see.'

'Ah, don't be mentioning that, Mammy, or I'll not come to lunch. And you can tell Moira yourself. She's right here.' Aisling passed the phone to her sister and she and Quinn took themselves off in search of a full Irish breakfast.

'Mammy, what's my cut of last night's take?' Moira demanded, taking a pew on the vacated sofa. She leaned her back against the arm rest and stretched her legs out so they were resting in the warm spot Aisling had left behind. There'd been no squeaking bed springs this morning on account of Aisling's sore head but still and all, she was warming to the idea of moving in with Tom. She liked the idea of opening her eyes each morning and seeing his face. What she didn't like was getting the evil eye from his swotty flatmates because they thought she was freeloading by staying over all the time. She'd been on the receiving end of one such look this morning as she'd left Tom to his studies earlier on. Any extra money she could lay her hands on would go into her flat-sharing fund, which was why she had her palm out now, figuratively speaking.

'Nothing. You worked for love. It's what families do, Moira.' Maureen was extremely pleased with how the evening had gone, Aisling's unfortunate flashing aside. They'd made a tidy profit.

'They don't and I didn't. I want paying, Mammy, and I want to make sure it's your treat today too before I promise I'm coming.'

Maureen huffed down the line. 'I'll see what I can do but only if you promise not to show me up at lunch today. You're to wear trousers, the Mo-pant if you want, but none of the knicker flashing skirts' you're so fond of. Do ya hear me?'

'I hear ya.'

Maureen got off the phone banging out Roisin's number next. Her voice was thick with sleep when she answered.

'Rise and shine, Roisin, you've an important lunch to be getting ready for and I want you looking presentable, not like you've been doing the riding all night long.'

'Mammy!' Roisin made to protest but when she put a hand to her hair, knew she had a point. It was a matted mess and would need to be dealt with.

'One o'clock at Johnnie Fox's.'

'I know, Shay's dropping me there.'

'Don't be late.'

'I won't.'

Maureen put the phone back and moved over to where Pooh was gazing with a love-struck expression on his face at Peaches shivering out on the veranda. She petted him to soften her words. 'She's not coming in, Pooh. It wouldn't be proper.' It was time she got ready herself. She'd already decided to wear the blue wrap dress. It was the right amount of dressy without being over the top. She'd keep her make-up light, subtle, no bright lipsticks. Her stomach flip-flopped at the thought of meeting Donal's girls. What would they make of her? What would she make of them?

Chapter 26

THE ROADS WERE BUSY for a Sunday with a hurling match having been played somewhere and there were eejits driving home cheering and carrying on. Maureen had allowed an hour to get to Glencullen so as to be on the safe side. Her trusty little car wound its way up the quiet stone-walled laneways, lush with greenery, into the Dublin mountains. On a sunny day the drive was spectacular but today the windscreen wipers gave an occasional swish to remove the light drizzle falling steadily outside.

She reached the picturesque pub with fifteen minutes to spare and pulled into the gravelled parking area over to the side of the cottagey building, grateful to find a space to slide into. Once she'd parked, she looked about to see if she could spy Donal's car. Her view to her right was blocked by a shuttle bus; the place was popular with the tourists and she should know having recommended it to her guests many times over the years. There was no sign of Donal's car or anybody else with whom she might link arms in solidarity. Aisling and Moira were getting a lift from Tom who must be getting thoroughly sick of playing chauffeur to the O'Mara girls and their entourage she thought. She'd give it five minutes and pretend she was very busy doing something important on her phone while she waited.

She was engaged in looking busy and never heard the footsteps approaching, nearly jumping out of her skin at the tap on the window. Moira was standing there jigging about in the cold air despite having dressed sensibly compared to her usual standards. Aisling was behind her, hands thrust in her coat pockets, white puffs of air coming from her mouth, looking very green around the gills. Maureen got out of the car, her coat falling open as she did so.

'I've not seen that dress before,' said Moira.

'It's a wrap dress. It sucks me in here,' Maureen gestured to her middle. 'Ciara at the shop I bought it from says so.'

'The colour's nice on you, Mammy.' Moira was doing her fecky brown-noser bit, not because she was a reformed character but to ensure a free lunch. Mammy would never know she'd told Aisling moments ago she felt like Cinders about to meet the ugly stepsisters. Aisling had been phlegmatic, saying they probably felt as though they were about to meet their evil stepmother. She had a point, Moira had thought, but now she feigned amazement. 'And sure, Mammy, you've no sign of a waist on you at all, Ciara was right.' That could have been overdoing it, she thought, seeing her eyes narrow.

Maureen looked past Moira to her other daughter. 'Aisling, good to see you've put your bosoms away today. How's the head?'

'Ah, don't, Mammy. I'm scarlet so I am and it's better than it was.' Mrs Baicu had been far more sympathetic than Mammy had earlier and had served her and Quinn a plate of Ireland's finest each, which had gone a long way to ensuring she didn't crawl back to bed.

'Come on,' Moira urged. 'My hair's going to kink standing around out here.' She led the charge past the wooden sign swinging in the breeze welcoming them to Ireland's highest pub, to where two children were charging around the outdoor tables playing tag, oblivious to the drizzle. The tables were deserted given the weather and a girl with a wave of blonde hair posed against the black vintage car parked alongside the pub as her boyfriend, presumably, took her photo. The brilliant purples and pinks cascading over the sides of the hanging baskets brightened a dull day and they stepped over the threshold of the quaint, lime-washed stone pub. The door closed behind them and they were instantly enveloped by the smell of browning butter and onions and the comforting sound of mellow laughter. Maureen looked up at the low ceiling and imagined Donal would have to duck if he didn't want to hit his head on the beams.

'Is Rosi here? Shay was going to drop her off,' Aisling asked, craning her neck, looking around but despite her heels she still couldn't see overtop of the punters clustered around in groups.

'I don't think so.' Moira replied.

Donal waved out from a table near the stage area which was deserted today. It was a good thing, Maureen thought. She wasn't able for Irish dancing not today. Her stomach was doing enough of a jig as it was. She had a split second to contemplate the two women sitting with him, older versions of the teenagers immortalised on his living room wall, before he was out of his seat and making his way through the crowded space to where the O'Mara women were hovering by the bar.

'Maureen,' he boomed, leaning in to kiss her on the cheek. Then, taking a step back, he looked from Aisling to Moira who'd been put on the back foot by the effusive greeting. 'Now then with that gorgeous hair, I'm going to guess, you're Aisling.'

Aisling nodded. She didn't know what she'd expected Donal to be like but he was a big teddy bear of a man. Handsome too, in a big teddy bear sorta way. He'd clasped hold of her hand and was shaking it warmly before turning his attention to Moira.

Moira's eyes flashed in a silent challenge for him to get it right and she sensed Mammy stiffen next to her, willing her to behave herself. 'And of course, you're Moira. Your mammy said you'd a look of Demi Moore about you. How do you do?' He gave her hand a pat between his big bear paw. It was warm and dry which gave him some kudos because Moira couldn't stand a sweaty palm. He was nothing like Daddy to look at, she mused, drinking in the sight of him curiously but he did remind her of someone. Someone famous but she couldn't put her finger on it. She liked his eyes, she decided; they were twinkly, maybe it was Father Christmas he reminded her of, he had a beard and twinkly eyes. She didn't get to ponder this further though because Roisin popped up alongside her like a jack-in-the-box.

'And I'm Rosi.' She took Donal's hand and shook it. 'Pleased to meet you. I'm not late I hope?'

'Not at all, Rosi. I've heard all about you, and Maureen was after telling me you can stand on your head and everything. Not to mention you've a fine young son.'

'I can and I have, yes, Noah, he's five.'

'Well, Maureen, you've three beautiful girls. No wonder you're so proud of them.' Donal beamed at each of them.

Maureen looked from one to the other of her three daughters, the mother hen, who was indeed proud of her chicks.

Chapter 27

DONAL CLAPPED HIS HANDS and in that big voice of his suggested they join him at their table so as he could introduce them to Louise and Anna. 'They're looking forward to meeting you all and then we can get the drinks in.' He'd taken charge, for which Maureen was grateful. He'd also taken hold of her hand in order to steer her over to the table to where his daughters were waiting. She could feel her girls' eyes on her back soaking in the strange sight of their mammy holding hands with a man they'd only just met. The flash of disapproval at their father's gesture on the face of the younger of the two women, Anna, didn't escape her notice either and she shivered in trepidation.

Donal made the introductions and Louise who was the eldest by two years nodded her hellos to the O'Mara group, the curiosity on her face plain to see. Anna did so too, although her expression was guarded as she sized them all up. There was a lot of silent looking up and down one another as Maureen took her coat off and hung it on the back of the chair next to where Donal had been seated. He pulled it out for her and she sat down. She now knew what the saying 'cat on a hot tin roof' meant, because jumpy and skittish was exactly how she felt and she didn't know what to do with her hands.

Louise, she saw, surreptitiously looking across the table at her, wore her hair short which gave her a no-nonsense, schoolteacher air. She gave the impression of being the sort of woman who'd be on committees and lots of them which, according to Donal, she was. She had her father's grey eyes and Maureen found comfort in that. She planned on talking to her about her children, a boy and a girl and for the life of her she couldn't remember their names which was ridiculous given Donal talked about them all the time. Her mind had gone blank due to her jangling nerves.

It was Anna who was making her nervous. You'd never guess Louise and Anna were sisters, at least not to look at. Mind, the same could be said about Aisling with her fair skinned colouring as compared to the rest of the family. Anna was small and fine boned with fussy, particular movements. Her hair was a soft blonde and sat on her shoulders flicking out at the ends. Donal had told her she'd struggled more than Louise with the loss of Ida. She'd been a mammy's girl and where Louise had the distraction of a full and busy life, juggling work and raising a family, Anna was an emergency room physician, a demanding role that didn't leave room, she said, for relationships. She looked fragile, Maureen thought, trying and failing to picture her taking charge in a hospital emergency room. Looks could be deceiving though and she hastily averted her eyes lest she get caught staring.

The walls around them were decorated with everything from framed newspaper cuttings, road signs and photographs, including one of Bill Clinton enjoying a pint here in the pub. The sense of good times had was imprinted in them all. Donal, who'd yet to sit down, had waited until everyone was seated before announcing he'd get the drinks from the bar. He took the orders repeating them slowly to try to remember who wanted what. Anna shot out of her seat. 'I'll help you, Dad.'

Louise looked trapped but she couldn't very well get up as well.

Maureen smiled over at her, wanting to put her at ease, but for a woman who was never short of things to say she was suddenly tongue-tied.

Roisin leaped in. 'I'm over from London for the weekend, Louise. My son's staying with his father.'

Louise grabbed hold of the conversation starter, eager not to sit in awkward silence. 'How old is he?'

'Five.' Roisin told her a little about Noah before asking if she had children. Louise gave them all the run down on her two, Brodie and Katie, making them laugh as she described the mayhem, they'd caused earlier that morning when they'd let their pet rabbits out of their hutch and they'd promptly hopped off on a neighbourhood sabbatical.

'I spent all morning trying to find them.' She rolled her eyes.

'And did you?' Roisin asked.

'I did, but only because Mrs Grenfall who lives at the end of the street telephoned my husband to say she had two rabbits fine-dining in her vegetable patch.'

Everybody laughed and the tension hovering over their table dissipated.

'Has Noah any pets?' Louise asked.

Roisin nodded. 'Yes, Mr Nibbles, his gerbil and he dotes on him.' She shared the story of how Mr Nibbles had decided her ex-mother-in-law's bra made a lovely bed, and the fuss she'd made upon finding Mr Nibbles nestling in the cup of her best bra.

They were all giggling when Donal put a round of drinks down in front of them with a pleased expression at the joviality around the table. Anna, carrying two wine glasses slid one towards her sister and shot her a glance as though to say, *traitor!*

She was going to be a tough nut to crack, Maureen thought, sighing into her wine glass.

Donal asked how the yoga pant party had gone and Moira piped up.

'They're called the Mo-pant now, aren't they, Mammy? It's short for Maureen not Moira in case you're wondering.'

Maureen gave Moira a warning look. 'We sold out. The party was a success.'

'What's this all about?' Louise asked, her curiosity piqued as Anna nursed her glass close to her chest.

The mood as Maureen relayed the story as to how they'd doctored the wine bottles was good-humoured and relaxed by the time the young lad waiting tables came over with his pen and pad in hand. Even Anna seemed a little more at ease. There was a mass opening of menus with Moira the first to order, Anna the last.

'So, these pants, Maureen, they're super comfortable you say?' Louise asked.

Maureen nodded. 'They are. Aren't they girls?'

The O'Mara sisters nodded and all three crossed their fingers under the table. The same thought running through their heads, *please God don't let her take it upon herself to get up and do a line dance demonstration,* but then remembering she wasn't wearing her Mo-pants they uncrossed them once more.

'Would I be able to order a pair?' Louise asked, to all their surprise.

Maureen looked to Roisin. 'Rosi's my supplier.'

'We sold out, Louise, but I'd be happy to post you a pair when I get home.'

'Grand. Let me know how much and I'll fix you up before we leave.'

'And I'll get your address.' Rosi smiled across the table having made up her mind she liked her.

Maureen risked a glance at Anna whose face was inscrutable. She chewed her bottom lip and then decided to try her luck instigating a conversation because she was nothing if not one of life's tryers and God loved a tryer.

'Anna, your dad's after telling me what an important job you have at the hospital. Anna's an emergency room physician.' She told Roisin, Aisling and Moira who made various utterances of 'really?' and 'oh wow'.

Anna nodded.

She could have been chewing on a clove given the look on her face, Roisin thought. If she was her sister, she'd be putting the boot in under the table.

'You do some long hours, don't you, love?' Donal coaxed.

Anna shrugged, not meeting anyone's gaze as she held the stem of her wine glass. 'People keep having emergencies.'

Moira asked, 'Is it like ER, you know, with your man Clooney?'

Anna was scornful as she replied, 'No, it's nothing like that.'

A tenseness settled over the table once more and this time it was Donal who chipped away at it by enquiring how Moira was getting on at college. 'She's a very good artist,' he told his girls. 'Maureen's shown me a painting you did which won the

Texaco Children's Art competition. It was very good. Of a fox it was.'

'Foxy Loxy,' Moira informed them.

'Mr Fox,' Aisling said.

'He's our resident fox at O'Mara's. He's a hole he squeezes through from the Iveagh Gardens behind the guesthouse in order to visit the bin outside our kitchen. It drives Mrs Flaherty, the breakfast cook, up the wall because he more often than not leaves a trail of rubbish behind to let her know he's paid a visit. She's always threatening to storm the gardens with her rolling pin.'

There was laughter at the image invoked and then Louise asked about the guesthouse, commenting on what a gorgeous example of Georgian architecture it was, not to mention its fabulous location. 'Dad told me you all grew up there. It must have been interesting, what with the different guests coming and going.'

'Well, we didn't know any different but I suppose it was,' Aisling spoke up for the first time as she described their games of hide and seek and how she'd tuck herself away in the dumbwaiter running all the way from their apartment on the top floor to the basement kitchen in order to read in peace. 'St Stephen's Green across the way was our garden,' she added. 'You can see the treetops from our living room window and I love to watch the leaves changing with the seasons.'

'And you manage it now?' Louise asked.

'I do, I love the place, and our guests. There's never a dull moment. I can't imagine living anywhere else now.'

'And you're a newly-wed?'

'Ah, Sweet Jesus,' said Moira. 'Don't be getting her started on that.' She winced as Mammy kicked her under the table.

The food began to arrive then, steaming plates of poached or pan-fried fish and Dublin Bay prawn deliciousness. They tucked in, all exclaiming over the buttery fish or silky sauce and the like before Maureen enquired as to what Louise's husband did, knowing it was something unpronounceable and interesting that took him away from home on occasion and involved dinosaur bones.

She filled them in on his role as a palaeontologist and the latest dig he was working on in Argentina.

'That must be hard, him being away for chunks of time like that,' Roisin said.

'The hardest thing is adjusting to him being back. Oh, don't get me wrong,' The flaky white fish wobbled on her fork which was poised midway between plate and mouth. 'I love my husband dearly but the children and I settle into routines when he's gone. We have to or we wouldn't get by, but when he gets home those routines go out the window and we all have to readjust once more.'

Roisin nodded in understanding.

By the end of the meal all the plates were almost licked clean, apart from Anna's, she'd barely touched her food or spoken. Any questions directed at her had been answered with the minimum number of words.

Moira looked at her sitting there all lemony lipped. This situation wasn't easy for any of them and sure, she'd been looking forward to lunch today as much as she would a visit to the dentist for a root canal. Nevertheless, she'd made an effort. To her complete amazement she'd found herself warming to

Donal despite her prior conviction she'd detest him on sight. She suspected it was on account of the Father Christmas thing. How could you dislike Father Christmas? Anna's expression throughout their meal had suggested someone had broken wind. Mammy was trying and it was making Moira cringe inside each time her forced cheeriness was rebuffed by Anna. It wasn't fair of her to treat Mammy as if she was something unpleasant on the sole of her shoe. She didn't deserve it and she'd had enough.

It was time somebody took matters into their own hands.

Chapter 28

DESSERT WAS DISHED out and being devoured when Anna mumbled her excuses and got up from the table in order to visit the Ladies. Moira carried on eating her Eton mess for a moment and then pushed her chair back saying she needed the bathroom. Maureen watched her go, it hadn't escaped her notice Anna had vacated her seat a few seconds earlier. She wondered what Moira was up to but there wasn't much she could say without causing a scene, and besides the lure of her whiskey cake was calling her to stay put and eat up.

Moira followed the sign, protruding from the wall, directing her to the Ladies and pushed open the door. There was only one occupied cubicle and she waited with her arms folded across her chest beside the hand drier. The loo flushed and Anna exited, her mouth forming an 'O' as she saw Moira standing there like an interrogator for the secret police.

'Is there a problem?' she asked, finding her words.

Moira softened her stance. She didn't want a pistols drawn at high noon scenario. She let her arms fall to her sides and said, 'Anna, I know you don't know me and I don't know you but I can tell you love your dad as much as I love my mammy.'

Anna's face was closed as she soaped up her hands. 'I don't know what you think you're doing, Moira, isn't it, accosting me in here like this.'

'I wanted a word was all. Nobody's accosting anybody.'

Anna didn't look convinced. 'Well, go on then, say your piece.'

Moira cleared her throat; she decided to just go with whatever came out of her mouth. 'When I found out Mammy had been dating someone, I wasn't happy. I wasn't ready for it. My daddy was my world and I'd thought he was Mammy's world too. It seemed,' she shrugged, trying to find the right words. 'Disloyal, I suppose, her even entertaining the idea of stepping out with another man.'

Anna ran the tap, rinsing her hands. She didn't say a word but at least she was listening, Moira thought, taking her cue to carry on. 'You know, I came to lunch today expecting not to like your dad but I saw the way he treats Mammy with respect and clearly enjoys being around her. Her face glows every time he talks to her. I love her and I don't want her to be lonely and the bottom line is, she has been lonely without Daddy and he's not coming back. I suppose I've decided over lunch just now, if she thinks your dad is wonderful then I owe it to her to get to know him.'

Anna moved her hands out from under the tap and it stopped running. She turned to face Moira and a tear slid down her cheek. Moira thought she looked very young and vulnerable but knew her to be older than she was. Her voice wobbled as she spoke. 'You know, in my line of work you'd think I'd be used to the fragility of life. I see people in unfathomable states every day and sometimes I can't patch them up and they die but I don't see the aftermath. I don't see the impact losing their loved one has on the people sitting in the hospital waiting room. Or, how they deal with their loss in the weeks, or months following. I wasn't ready to lose my mum.'

'Was it sudden?' Moira didn't know how Donal's wife had passed.

Anna nodded. 'She had a heart attack behind the wheel of her car and died instantly. Small mercy no one else was hurt when she crashed. I've had no idea how to handle it and I don't know how I'm supposed to be anymore. The rug's been ripped out from under my feet and Dad's my one constant.'

Moira didn't think, she acted, and stepping forward she embraced Anna. To her surprise it was returned and she felt her body shuddering as she sobbed. 'Anna, that's how I felt, too. Daddy was my safety net. I knew I could screw up and he'd pick me up and put me back on the right path again because he always did. I didn't deal well with his passing. It's why I don't drink anymore.'

They broke apart a little embarrassed by the intimacy and Anna ducked into the cubicle she'd exited and tore off some toilet paper, she passed a wad to Moira so she could blow her nose too. She dabbed her eyes, and wiped her nose before saying, 'I want Dad to be happy, of course I do. It's just, I thought me and Louise and the children were enough.'

'I thought the same.' Moira tossed the soggy paper in the bin. 'I couldn't understand why Mammy needed anyone else. She's us and plenty of friends to be getting about with but with Donal it's different.'

'I need to let Dad move on, don't I?'

Anna was seeking confirmation and Moira wondered in that instant how she managed such a responsible role at the hospital. She had to be so much stronger than she looked. 'I think we both need to understand we're not losing our mam and daddy all over again, because they'll always be with us, here.' She put her hand on her heart. 'But maybe we're going to gain some new friends. I'm hoping so.' Her smile was tentative.

Anna blinked at this girl standing uncertainly in front of her. She was extremely pretty and she'd pigeon holed her as an airhead on sight but she was anything but. 'I'd like that, too.'

She turned then to look in the mirror. 'We'd better be getting back or they'll be thinking we're after having fisticuffs. Jaysus, I look like I've been in the ring with one of the Fury's.'

'Here,' Moira opened her bag and retrieved a cotton bud from her cosmetic purse. 'This'll do the trick.'

'Thanks. I can't wear waterproof mascara, my eyes are too sensitive.' She set about using the bud to wipe the smudged black streaks from under her eyes and then, satisfied she was as good as she was going to get, said, 'Come on then. I'm wishing I'd ordered dessert now.'

'You can share mine,' Moira said, holding the door open.

Chapter 29

BRONAGH HAD HUMMED and hawed over wearing her new Mo-pants to church. She was worried she'd be on the receiving end of a disapproving look from Father Kilpatrick for being too casual in her dress. The conundrum was, she was feeling rather bloated and couldn't face the thought of sitting like an overstuffed garden gnome for the duration of the service. The reason for this state of affairs was because she'd helped clear up what was left of the lovely nibbly finger food on offer at the party last night along with a woman named Joan. Her skirt had been very short given the weather and Bronagh had been pleased to hear she'd bought a pair of Mo-pants herself. They'd be far more appropriate for her to be gadding about in. Comfort was key she'd decided in the end and so had teamed the pants with an oversized teal sweater and matching scarf.

As it happened, there was no such look forthcoming from Father Kilpatrick and she'd had more than one tap on the shoulder to tell her how well she looked. Mam too had enjoyed the choice of hymns today and was still humming now as she finished off her scrapbook project. She was a proper songbird was Mam. She always said, no matter how she was feeling within herself music had the power to lift her soul. She'd have to get her a pair of the Mo-pants too, Bronagh decided. If she'd wear them that was. She wasn't a trouser woman, she preferred her skirts. She'd think on it.

The phone rang as Bronagh peeled the lid back from a tin of tomato soup. She'd picked up a loaf of fresh bread to go with it for lunch on their way home. She'd lost track of the time she saw, glancing at the wall clock and realising it was midday. Hilary rang every Sunday to speak to Mam at twelve o'clock on the dot and so she put the tin down and went to answer the phone. There was no point in seeing to lunch until Mam had finished her chat.

'Hello?' she asked, even though she knew who it was.

'Bronagh, it's Hilary. How's your week been?'

'Grand.' She debated telling her sister about the party she'd been to last night but decided not to. From experience she knew Hilary, the queen of one-upmanship, would cut her off mid-flow to tell her about her new dress or coat or whatever. No, she decided, swallowing back the story, she wouldn't allow herself to feel miffed by her sister not when she was in such a sunny mood. Instead, she fibbed and said, 'I'll pass you over to Mam, Hilary. I've soup on the stove and it's about to boil over.

She took the phone in for her mam who put the glue she'd been about to stick to the back of a tiny cardboard flower down on the tray table along with the rest of her materials. She sat up in her chair expectantly and took the telephone from Bronagh. She looked forward to hearing all Hilary's news each week. Bronagh went back to the kitchen and sat down at the table. A cloud had passed over the sun just as it had her mood, despite her best intentions. Hilary's voice had brought the past knocking once more.

1971

Bronagh hung her new coat in her wardrobe. She'd bought it in Brown Thomas on her way home from work. The rich, burgundy colour and smart gold buttons had drawn her over to the mannequin displaying it and she'd known it was perfect for her trip to Donegal. She'd tell a while lie if her mam asked where it was from, she'd tell her Arnotts. She was still loyal to her old place of employment even now. Her wardrobe for the weekend in the north was now complete. She'd new trousers and a gorgeous cream sweater too. She was going for a shampoo and set on Friday straight from work which would still give her time to organise the taxi to take her mam to the station.

She hugged herself, barely able to contain her fizzing excitement about the impending break, not just because she was going to meet Kevin's family but because of the change of scenery. She was so looking forward to being somewhere different, sniffing the Donegal air and exploring the sights to be seen through adult eyes. The last time she'd been up that way, she'd been a child with no interest in anything other than, would there be swimming and would they be allowed an ice cream? It would do both her and Mam the world of good to have a couple of days away from home, she thought, picking up her mam's habit and humming to herself.

She heard the door go downstairs followed by muffled voices below her. Kevin was here for his tea. She'd a lovely corned beef simmering in the pot and would serve it with a generous dollop of cabbage and mashed potato. Kevin liked her mash. He'd even gone so far as to tell her it was better than his mam's which was high praise indeed. Bronagh knew how much he missed her home cooking. She'd told him it was down to her secret ingredient. He'd pressed her but she refused to divulge it because she didn't want him passing it on to his mam and sisters. The mash was her pièce de résistance as the French would say! Butter, and lots of it, was the key to flavour when it came to tasty cooking but what made her potato side dish stand out was the sprinkle of garlic powder she added. Another nod to the French.

Bronagh ran a brush through her hair and freshened her lipstick in her dressing table mirror before closing her bedroom door and taking to the stairs two at a time. Kevin was in the front room talking to her mam. He turned when she walked in and flashed her a grin which still had the effect of making her knees go weak. She knew a grin was all she'd get too. He was far too polite to kiss her in front of her mam who was sitting forward in her chair waiting for him to tell her about his day.

She smiled back at him and left them to chat as she went to put the potatoes on. She was chopping the cabbage when she felt his arms snake around her waist before he planted a kiss on her cheek.

'How're you, gorgeous?'

'Grand.'

'What's for dinner.'

'Corned beef, mash and cabbage.'

'I was hoping you'd say that, and will you be making the gravy I like too?'

'I might be. You'll have to wait and see,' she teased, before shaking him off. 'Now don't be distracting me or there'll be no dinner for anyone.'

'I came in for the sherry bottle.'

'You know where it is,' Bronagh said, pointing the knife in her hand to the cupboard where the bottle of sweet sherry was kept. Myrna had taken to enjoying a small tot when Kevin came for his tea. He retrieved it, then helped himself to a can from the fridge. Bronagh always made sure she had a couple in for when he called. He lifted the tab and she heard the phfft of gas being released. He fetched a glass and poured the contents into it, knowing Myrna would disapprove of him drinking straight from the can.

There was laughter around the kitchen table that evening as Kevin told them a tale about a woman who'd gone out to collect the milk still at the gate well after ten that morning, in her dressing gown and slippers, only to have the door snip shut behind her. She'd had to go to the neighbours and wait there for him to come. She'd been mortified, he said.

'Was it a housecoat sorta dressing gown, you know the type they wear in the films with the heeled fluffy, kitten slippers?' Bronagh asked tongue-in-cheek, doubting there were many women in the Dublin suburbs who got around of a morning dressed like Hollywood film stars.

'No, it was not. It was a tatty old thing.'

That made her giggle.

'Serves her right for not getting dressed in the first place,' Myrna piped up. She prided herself on always getting dressed, even on her worst days, if she made it down the stairs. 'This meat's lovely, Bronagh. Melt in your mouth.'

The telephone shrilling made them all jump and Bronagh resented the intrusion into their pleasant evening but she couldn't very well leave it unanswered. She answered it on the third ring. 'Hello?'

'Bronagh, it's Hilary.'

Her sister's voice turned the meal she'd been enjoying into a solidified lump in the pit of her stomach. She wouldn't be phoning to chat about the weather. Not wanting the rest of the evening spoiled, she tried to head her off. 'Hilary, can I call you back we're just having our tea.'

'No, listen, I won't keep you. I'm ringing to apologise because there's to be a change of plan this weekend. We can't have Mammy to stay because Erin's after catching the flu and you know how susceptible Mammy is. She couldn't possibly be around her.'

Bronagh's chest tightened at the crushing disappointment of it all and if her mam and Kevin weren't sitting a stone's throw away, she'd have burst into messy, noisy tears at the unfairness of it all. As it was, she kicked the carpet, glad of the pain in her toe to distract from the pain in her heart.

Chapter 30

MAUREEN AND DONAL WALKED past the middle pier where the Howth Yacht Club was located, both rugged up in hats, scarfs and coats, arm in arm. Pooh was leading the charge, snuffling his way along the pavement. They paused, much to Pooh's chagrin, to look at the curve of the white building with its glassed-in balcony wrapping around it. A blue and white striped awning hovered over it protectively, reminding them the summer months would eventually roll around again. For now though, it was deserted, but in a few months when the weather warmed up, the long, narrow space would be filled with members observing the action in the harbour. The abandoned, moored yachts bobbed in the grey waters of the Irish Sea alongside it, their masts stark white against the sombre sky. Maureen was looking forward to continuing her sailing lessons come the summer and wondered if she might be able to talk Donal into learning too.

'To think that's where we met,' he shouted over the wind. They both stood there, lost in the memory of their first encounter. Maureen had been at the yacht club Christmas party, an event she'd been looking forward to until she'd wound up sandwiched between two eejits at the dinner table. Donal and his band were the entertainment and she'd escaped for a dance, their eyes had locked, and the rest was, as they say, history. Donal squeezed her arm. 'I thought you a fine-looking woman in your red dress the moment I saw you step onto the dance floor, Maureen O'Mara.'

Maureen smiled up at him. 'I thought you had a look of Kenny Rogers about you alright and I always thought he was a fine-looking man.'

They stared at one another in mutual admiration until Pooh began to strain at the leash, eager for the off. Maureen's step was lighter this morning after their luncheon at Johnnie Fox's yesterday, although given what she'd eaten it had no right to be. The lunch had started off promising to be a disaster but it had all turned around over dessert and they'd left the pub with promises of doing it again soon and two orders for the Mo-pants to boot. She didn't know what had been said in the Ladies Room between Anna and Moira but they'd rejoined them at the table giggling over a private joke and Maureen had blinked in disbelief as Moira passed Anna a spoon and Anna began to share her dessert with her. This was remarkable, not just because Anna seemed to have undergone a personality transformation in the powder room, but because Moira by nature was not a sharer. All in all, the family meet-up had been a success. It was baby steps for them all in these new unchartered waters but the first big storm had been averted and they'd sailed into calmer waters. It was the Irish Sea and the sight of Ireland's eye out there making her all metaphorical, Maureen decided.

Roisin had gone back to London last night but before she'd left, they'd had a board meeting as to how they could fill the orders streaming in. When they'd gotten back to the apartment after lunch on the Sunday there'd been a ton of messages left on the answerphone from women requesting a pair of the Mo-pants because so and so had told them they were marvellous.

There was a comfy pant revolution going on in Ireland to be sure. The plan so far was for Roisin to add postage to the orders and send them directly to the customer. There was definitely scope for another Tupperware, Mo-pant style party in the future. Given Moira's recent good deed with Anna and Aisling's boob aberration, Moira might find herself promoted to the role of Mo-pant glamour girl next time around.

Pooh cocked a leg and they halted once more. Donal greeted a chap with a rod slung over his shoulder and a bucket of something smelly for catching fish in his hand. They embarked on a great chat as to what could be found here in the harbour if you had a lucky spot as yer man with the smelly bucket did. She stood politely, waiting for the conversation to come to a natural close, pleased Pooh hadn't shown them up by deciding to do a number two when they had company. Her mind flitted to Patrick. She'd taken it upon herself to telephone him. Sure, someone had to. He'd been delighted to hear from her and she'd held the phone away from her ear wondering if this man with an accent that had picked up more than one Americanism was really her son. She'd felt a longing to tousle his hair and wrap him in a hug the way she'd done when he was a boy. It was high time she got over there to Los Angeles to see where he was living for herself.

For Patrick's part he'd been full of his new venture which involved investing in something that went completely over the top of Maureen's head. If things were going well, it boded well for him paying back his loan and the last burden resting on Maureen's shoulders had lifted. She'd never doubted him. She'd asked after Cindy before hanging up, even though she was on the fence as to her suitability as a long-term prospect for her

beloved eldest son. Apparently, she was becoming sought after in the world of toothpaste adverts. Patrick had insisted on
putting her on and Maureen had nearly choked when Cindy,
in that breathy, little girl voice of hers had said, 'Hi, Mom, how
are you?'

She realised Donal had said cheerio to the chap, who was
whistling as he carried on his way to his lucky spot, and they set
off walking once more. This time Maureen squeezed his arm.
She was a lucky woman, truly blessed with her lot in life.

Chapter 31

MAUREEN EYEBALLED PEACHES without realising she was doing so. The cat was taunting her as she sat outside on the balcony table daring her to shoo her away. She was oblivious to the fact Maureen might as well have been staring at a brick wall because she was lost in thought not engaging in a staring competition. Pooh was sitting by her feet enraptured by the Persian who again was oblivious to the poor dog's adoration. Donal was in the kitchen chopping an onion having insisted on cooking his world-famous, in Drumcondra at least, spaghetti bolognaise for their dinner. He was crooning along to a country music compilation he'd brought with him for Maureen and Pooh to have a listen to. Maureen registered the sharp smack of onion as she blinked and Peaches stretched, languorously satisfied, she was the winner of the competition.

She turned away from the window and mooched into the kitchen, picking up a piece of the tomato Donal had already chopped. He refused to use canned tomatoes for his sauce. She popped the segment in her mouth and chewed, she was feeling decidedly unblessed at this moment in time thanks to Aisling.

She, Donal and Pooh had all tumbled in through the door, glad to be back in the warmth after their bracing stroll and she'd seen the blinking light of the answerphone. 'I wonder if that's more orders for the Mo-pants,' she'd said, before directing Donal to the kitchen to put the kettle on. She replayed the messages, hastily scribbling down two new orders and then frowning as Aisling's voice sounded. Her tone was snippy as she demanded her mammy telephone her back as soon as she got the message. Maureen would have been worried but she didn't sound panicked, more annoyed and so, expecting to have to mediate the latest battle between Moira and Aisling she'd taken a deep breath and rung back.

Now, Donal put the knife down and said, 'Come on, Maureen, you're miles away. Why don't you tell me what the problem is?' She watched as he washed his hands and poured them both a glass of red. 'The dinner can wait a while longer. C'mon let's sit down.' He handed her a glass and she followed his lead over to the sofa. Sitting down, he patted the seat beside him. Maureen obliged and, taking a sip of her wine, she savoured the bold, meaty flavour before relaying Aisling's side of the telephone conversation he hadn't been privy to.

'Aisling, what's got you all in a stew?' she'd asked when her daughter picked up.

'You have, Mammy. I can't believe you're after loaning money to Patrick. You know what he's like.'

Maureen had sat down; she hadn't expected that. 'Aisling, I don't know what you're on about.' The fib tripped off her tongue. Surely Bronagh wouldn't have repeated their chat?

'Yes, you do. Roisin overheard Patrick tapping you for ten thousand pounds at Christmas time and why she's taken this long to tell me and Moira about it, I don't know.' Roisin had telephoned Aisling that morning from work to tell her what she'd heard when neither Patrick or Mammy knew she was within earshot at Christmas. 'Why didn't you tell us when you were here, or over for my wedding?' Aisling had wanted to know.

'Because there was too much going on. There's always too much going on. I never got the chance to. But it's bothering me and you're better at broaching things like this with Mammy than I am,' Roisin replied, feeling much better now she'd unburdened herself.

'No, Rosi,' Aisling had told her. 'You just don't do confrontation on any level.' Roisin had hung up then on the pretext of urgent work she had to be getting on with, leaving Aisling with the phone in her hand and her blood boiling at the thought of her brother taking advantage of their mammy.

'Loan, Aisling, there's a big difference.' She should have known it would've been one of her three with their big flappy ears, not Bronagh, Maureen had thought, still taken aback to be even having this conversation.

'Aha, got you!'

She had walked into that one. Maureen was annoyed. There'd be no escaping this unpleasant conversation now unless she hung up. 'I don't see what business it is of yours or your sister's what I do with my money, Aisling.'

'Sure, Mammy, I know that but it's not me trying to get my hands on your retirement fund now, is it?'

'Your brother needed a buffer is all to get his new business off the ground. If you can't help family who can you help?' She'd felt Donal's concerned gaze on her and was embarrassed he should hear her sounding like a fishwife down the phone. She tried to level her voice out. 'Everybody deserves a helping hand from time to time.'

'Mammy, Patrick's had more helping hands than I've had hot dinners! The reason he needed to ask you for money is because he's got champagne tastes on beer money and he has the business sense of a flea to boot. Sure, he's like a fecking flea the way he bounces from one sure thing to another. He never sticks at anything long enough to make it work.'

'Aisling O'Mara, don't you be using the language or talking ill of your brother. I'll have you know he's doing very nicely over there in Los Angeles. His business is going great guns, so it is. I was only after speaking to him the other day and, for your information, I'm thinking of taking a holiday over there.' This time she'd known Donal's gaze would be startled. Hers had been just as startled by what had popped out of her mouth. She'd not even realised she was seriously entertaining the idea, but sure, why not?

'Oh, did Pat offer to pay for this holiday? And did he mention a repayment plan to you during this conversation of yours?'

Maureen had thought she might get struck down by lightning if she fibbed twice. 'No, but only because we didn't get around to talking about it. Besides I gave him until Christmas to pay it back and that's months off yet.'

'Well more fool you, Mammy. Weren't you after telling me the other day about Great Aunt Noreen and the postcard she sent you from New York? And how you were worried Emer was taking advantage of her.'

Maureen squirmed. She had indeed been telling her how Emer, Noreen's canny niece who knew too well which side her bread was buttered, was taking advantage of her lonely old aunt. It wasn't the first time Emer had done so either, but loneliness was a powerful motivation to put your blinkers on where family was concerned. Was she guilty of the same thing? No, she decided, Patrick was her son. He wouldn't do wrong by her.

'Sure, there's no comparison. Patrick's not at all like Emer,' she'd said, knowing exactly when Aisling's distrust of her brother had taken root. It was when, shortly after Brian died, she'd given the family the ultimatum to either take over the running of the guesthouse or she'd be selling O'Mara's. Living with her memories and without her husband in the family apartment had become too much for her and she'd been desperate for a fresh start here in Howth. If they'd sold, the children would have got their inheritance early and Patrick had been desperate to offload the old place. He'd wanted to take his share of the proceeds of sale and put them into one of his entrepreneurial schemes. The other three had wanted the family business to stay in the family and Aisling, with her background in tourism, had stepped up and taken on the managerial role. Patrick's nose had been knocked firmly out of joint by the announcement Aisling would be taking over the day-to-day management of O'Mara's and he'd made sure they'd all known it.

Donal had put a cup of tea down on the side table next to where she was sitting then, and she'd been suddenly weary of the conversation knowing there was no resolution to be had. 'Aisling O'Mara. I'm only going to say this the once. I'll not be dictated to by any of you. Not yourself, Roisin, Moira or Patrick for that matter. I'm the mammy in this family and you'd do well to remember it.'

She finished telling Donal what had transpired and took another sip of her wine. She gave him a sidelong glance wondering if he'd think she'd been foolish where Patrick was concerned, just as she'd thought Noreen was for forking out so as Emer could have a fancy holiday.

'Maureen, it's not up to me to tell you what to do or to get involved in your family affairs. Patrick's your son and we always want to help our children to better themselves, it's what we do as parents. My only advice would be to talk to him if it's bothering you and put your mind at rest. We spend too much time worrying over things we could resolve if we only talked to one another. As for Aisling, I think now she's blown off steam she'll be back on the phone within the hour to apologise.'

'You're right, Donal,' Maureen said. Aisling wasn't a sulker. She smiled up at him feeling fortunate to have him here to listen to her family dramas and even more fortunate he had no intention of interfering.

'What I would like to know, though, is when you're planning on going to Los Angeles because you hadn't mentioned it?'

'I hadn't thought of it, not really. The other day when I spoke to Pat, I thought it would be lovely to go and see him over there in America, you know the way you do. The holiday thing just came out of my mouth.'

Donal chortled. 'Well, I don't mind telling you I wouldn't mind escaping the tail-end of this weather. Oh, yes, I could swap it for a few palm trees and a hotel with a pool.'

'You'd come with me?'

'If you'd have me.'

'I'd like that.'

They smiled at each other in mutual admiration once more.

Over at O'Mara's, Aisling was curled up on the sofa next to Moira. Moira had a face pack on and was picking poodle hair off her Mo-pants muttering on about that dog having been sitting on the furniture when no one was looking. She'd offered to give Aisling a facial too but after the last debacle where she'd used cheap shite on her and Aisling had wound up with hives for days, she'd told her to feck off with her face pack. Now, she turned to Moira and said, 'I still can't believe she hung up on me.'

Moira's setting green mask cracked as she spoke. 'I think you went too far and you know you're going to have to ring her back and apologise or Mammy will act the martyr.'

'Oh, pipe down, Shrek,' Aisling said, folding her arms across her chest and sliding down her seat in a sulk. She wasn't ready to ring back. She wasn't in the mood for criticism from Moira either. "Well, someone has to speak up where he's concerned or he'd walk all over her.'

'Mammy gave him until Christmas to pay her back, Ash, you jumped the gun telephoning her and giving out like so.'

Aisling chewed her lip, she loved her brother, of course she did, he was family but he was still slippery as an eel. Maybe just maybe she had been a tad hasty.

'I want to know more about this holiday of hers to Los Angeles. Do you think she might take us?' Moira asked.

'I'm a married woman, she'd have to take my husband too.'

'Feck off, Aisling,' Moira said. 'And ring Mammy.'

Aisling sighed, she wasn't a sulker and she hated going to sleep on a fight so she might as well get it over with, and picking up the phone, she pushed redial.

Chapter 32

THE WEEKS HAD TUMBLED over one another the way they do and as the days had passed, orders for the Mo-pants had dipped. Maureen had come to the reluctant conclusion, just as had happened with the Flower Power movement and other revolutions that had gone before, the comfy pants day was done. They'd had their moment in the sun and shone brightly but there were only so many women she could reach out to from here in Howth. Truth be told, she didn't feel inclined to undertake a nationwide tour to promote the Mo-pants either, not now she had Donal. Mind, if they did have a holiday over there in America, she might be tempted to take a few pairs over and see how the land lay. For now, though, it was gratification enough to see her fellow line dancing ladies stepping that little bit wider although she wished Rosemary Farrell would stop harping on about how she still couldn't lunge on account of her hip, Mo-pants or no Mo-pants.

Today, Maureen was having her final lesson with Maria before Saturday's big birthday bash where she'd be singing alongside Donal. They'd still not squeezed in an official practice with the rest of the band but she'd sung her two numbers with Donal every chance they got and was satisfied she was as ready as she'd ever be.

'Do you think we could run through the scales one last time, without the tambourine, Maureen?' Maria asked, looking up at her expectantly from her piano stool before smoothing her flowy skirt.

Maureen, who was standing in a puddle of sunlight which was making her feel as though she were spotlighted on stage, reluctantly put the tambourine down. Maria smiled her thanks, flexed her fingers and off they went running through their Do-Re-Mi-Fa-So-La-Ti-Do.

'Good, very good, Maureen,' Maria said when they'd finished. 'Now then, I managed to lay my hands on the sheet music for *We've got Tonight* and *Islands in the Stream*, shall we see how we get on with those?'

'We can't.' Maureen shook her head.

'Why not?'

'We've no Kenny and I can't be doing all three. It's not possible.'

Maria took a deep breath. She was a kind woman was Maureen O'Mara, a heart'o gold on her because hadn't she brought her a lovely dense porter cake today? The children would enjoy a slice of that for their afternoon tea and, given she didn't bake much, her husband would be in seventh heaven when he got to sit down for his evening supper with a wedge. She might even pop out later and get a bottle of cream to whip for him to have on the side. 'I'll be Kenny, Maureen,' she explained patiently, as though to a small child.

'But you're a woman.'

Maria dug her nails into her palms. 'I realise that, I've birthed three children, Maureen, but sure, we can improvise, can't we?'

'Do you have a white jacket you could put on?'

'Begging your pardon?'

'A white jacket. You know like Kenny wore, white trousers too, would be grand if you've any. I always think it's good to look the part, you know.'

'No, I'm sorry, Maureen, I don't.'

'Well then if you've no jacket and trousers can I use the tambourine? To get myself in the mood, like.' Her hand was already inching toward it.

'You can use the tambourine,' Maria said through gritted teeth.

'I suppose we could give it a try then.'

Maria knew she'd be laughing about this later when she relayed the tale to her husband over their porter cake and dollop of cream but right now she was summoning all the strength she had. 'Okay then, I think we'll start with *We've Got Tonight*.' She shuffled her sheet music until she found what she was looking for and placed it on the stand in front of her. 'All set?'

Maureen rattled her tambourine to signal she was ready as she'd ever be.

'Here we go.' Maria began to play the opening notes, launching into the song effortlessly.

Maureen was mesmerised and she missed her cue to join in. 'You're very good,' she said when Maria stopped playing to see what the issue was. 'If I shut my eyes, I could believe you were a man.'

'Why don't you shut your eyes then, Maureen.'

Maureen eyed Maria. Who'd have thought she'd have such a big man voice inside of that little chest. She also thought she'd detected a slight smart-arse tone in her voice just now, something she was well versed in thanks to her children. She let it go.

'We'll start at the top then, shall we?'

Maureen rattled the tambourine and Maria wished she could sit on her hands because she was sorely tempted to grab hold of it and throw it over the hedge outside.

This time, they ran through the whole song with Maria only feeling unnerved once when Maureen suddenly draped herself over the piano with a passionate look on her face as she did her Sheena bit.

Next, they rehearsed *Islands in the Stream* and this time there was no piano lounging although Maria did notice Maureen had sucked in her tummy and thrust her chest out in order to perform her version of Dolly.

'Well, Maureen,' Maria said, her hands resting on the keys. 'I think you're as ready as you'll ever be. That was great. You nailed both songs. You play the part very well. Song is just as much about performance as it is simply singing the lyrics.'

'Thanks a million, Maria. I've enjoyed these lessons so. But I'm not quite ready there's one more thing I need to do.'

'Oh, yes?' Maria held her breath in the hope there were no more Sheena, Dolly songs about to be requested.

'Yes. I need a stage outfit and there's a boutique down on the main street here where I think I'll be able to find just the thing.' Maureen could have worn her red Chinese silk dress she'd had made in Vietnam. She'd been wearing it the night she met Donal. Or, she could have worn her electric blue, wrap dress but she wanted something new. Something special to wear for what was going to be a very special occasion after all. Her debut performance.

'Good luck, Maureen. You'll make a grand Sheena so you will.'

'And Dolly, Maria. Don't forget Dolly.'

Chapter 33

'HELLO THERE, CIARA, how're ye today?' Maureen bustled inside the clothes shop with a brown paper bag in her hand. She put it down on the counter in front of the startled girl. 'I'm after bringing you in an egg sandwich for your lunch.'

'That's very kind of you.' Ciara blinked. Now she recalled who this random woman depositing food parcels on her counter was. She was the electric blue wrap dress lady who'd cast aspersions on her mammy for not feeding her.

'Not at all. Now then, when you've eaten, I'd like your help again with an outfit for a special occasion. The wrap dress has had lots of compliments.'

'Is someone getting married?' Ciara brightened, she loved helping her customers choose mother-of-the-bride or groom outfits.

'Jaysus wept, no! Sure, we've just got through one wedding in the family.'

'An anniversary then?' Ciara pulled the thick triangle of white bread and eggy mayonnaise from the bag and stared at it. It was enormous, three meals in one.

'No, I'm performing on Saturday night, on the stage like, at a seventieth birthday party and I'm after something with a country and western feel to it but it's got to be class, too, if you know what I mean.'

Ciara hadn't a clue but she was enjoying her sandwich.

'A word from the wise, Ciara.' Maureen said. 'Don't eat so fast or you'll give yourself the indigestion. I'll have a little browse about the place.'

Maureen busied herself looking at the different styles as the smell of egg drifted about the shop. It was very strong, she hadn't thought of that. Still and all, Ciara over there was virtually inhaling the thing. Poor love was half starved.

'I'll be with you in half a tick,' Ciara called over.

'Another word to the wise,' Maureen called back. 'Don't talk with your mouth full.' Sure, that girl's mam was a disgrace so she was, not feeding her and not teaching her any manners.

Maureen had pulled a dress she liked the look of off the rack and when Ciara had finally finished her sandwich she stalked over in heels, reminding Maureen of exactly that, a stalk.

'I enjoyed that, thank you.'

Maureen took a step back from the full-frontal egg breath assault. 'Not a bother. Now what do you think to this? She held up the red dress with the black belt trying to picture it with the white Stetson Laura had offered to loan her. She'd have to get some matching boots, she decided, not fancying her chances of sourcing a pair of white cowboy boots in Howth. A trip to the city would be needed.

'No, no, no. You'd look like Mrs Claus in that,' Ciara tutted, whisking it away and flicking through a colourful rack until she uttered a self-satisfied, 'Perfect.' She held it up for Maureen to see.

It was yellow and lacy with a sweetheart neckline and nipped-in waist, quite unlike anything Maureen had worn before. 'I'll look like Loretta Lyn in that.' She snatched it off Ciara who was about to ask who Loretta Lyn was, but Maureen was already locking the fitting room door whipping everything off in order to try it on.

'Are you ready?' she called out a minute later.

'Ready!'

Maureen unlocked the door and waltzed on to the shop floor with a swagger she felt was suitably countrified. 'Now, Ciara, I want you to pretend I'm wearing a white cowboy hat and I've matching boots on.'

Ciara nodded.

'What are you thinking?'

'I'm thinking you look like you're about to burst into a country and western song.'

It was exactly the response Maureen was hoping for. She made to leave the shop with her new yellow, lacy dress, wrapped in tissue paper tucked inside a bag with the boutique's name on it, when the door opened. She stepped aside to allow a woman with big black sunglasses pushed up on the top of her head, despite their being no sign of the sun anymore, over the threshold. Before she could venture forth however, Maureen laid a hand on her arm and leaned in to whisper. 'If you're wondering what the smell is in here, I want you to know it wasn't me or Ciara there behind the counter. She's after having an egg sandwich is all.' She'd hate for the woman to think badly of either of them.

Chapter 34

1971

BRONAGH DIDN'T WANT to tell her mam she wouldn't be spending the weekend in Tramore with Hilary and the family, after all. Not in front of Kevin. She'd stood in the hallway holding the phone in her hand, even though her sister was no longer on the other end, and taken a moment to compose herself. Her disappointment was like a big rock bearing down on her and she hoped it didn't show as she ventured back into the kitchen.

'Who was that on the phone ringing at teatime?' Myrna asked disapprovingly.

'Only Rhoda,' Bronagh fibbed, her friend's name the first that had sprung to mind. 'I told her I'd call her back later.'

'Rhoda should know better. Sit down and have your meal, Bronagh, before it gets cold,' her mam bossed. She was always livelier when Kevin was here, more like the mam of old. He was good for Mam just like he was good for her.

Bronagh glanced at his plate. He'd nearly cleaned his meal up and before she sat down, she offered him another sliver of the tender, salted meat carved on the chopping board.

'I won't say no.' He grinned and forked a slice on to his plate. 'And a smidge more gravy if there's any left.'

Pleased he was enjoying her meal she passed him the jug then sat down. Her appetite was gone but somehow, she managed to get the rest of what was on her plate down her. At least she hadn't loaded it up, wanting to make sure there was plenty for Kevin. Her trousers had been feeling on the snug side lately, she'd needed to cut back on her serving size. Mam ate like a bird most of the time but tonight she'd managed a decent helping which was good to see. The last mouthful lodged in her throat and she got up from the table quickly and fetched a glass of water to swallow it down with.

'You go and watch your programme, Myrna,' Kevin said as they all placed their knives and forks down. 'I'll help Bronagh wash up.'

'Ah, you're a grand lad, Kevin. Your mammy ought to be proud of you.' Myrna patted his arm and turned to Bronagh her eyes shining. 'That was a lovely meal.'

Bronagh's heart broke for her own disappointment and for her mam's as she watched her shuffle slowly back to the front room to settle in for her show.

'It was.' Kevin patted his middle. 'I'll be getting a belly on me if I don't watch it.' He rolled up his sleeves having proven himself to be a handy washer-upper while Bronagh dried and put the dishes away. As they toiled, he rambled on about all the places he'd take her to see around Donegal. The Slieve League cliffs, Ballymastocker Bay and, if they had time, they'd take the ferry to Arranmore Island. He pulled the plug from the sink and the water gurgled down the drain. His gaze when he turned it on Bronagh was quizzical. Her quietness since dinner hadn't escaped him but he didn't say anything, figuring Bronagh would tell him if something was bothering her. 'Shall we head down for a pint?' he asked cheerfully as she hung the tea towel over the oven door handle.

Bronagh nodded and went to fetch her coat from the hook in the hallway. She couldn't bring herself to wear her new one, not now, in fact she may as well take it back to the store given the tag was still attached. She popped her head in on her mam who was laughing at something on the television. She'd leave her tonight, tell her in the morning. 'Kevin and I are going for a drink down at the Four Horses, Mam. I'll be home later.'

'Enjoy yourselves.'

'G'night, Myrna.' Kevin called.

She held her hand up in an absentminded wave not wanting to miss a second of her programme and Kevin and Bronagh ventured out into the still night.

Powdery snow was falling, muffling the world around them. Bronagh wondered if it would settle or if it would be gone by morning as though it had never been there in the first place. Kevin's arm was draped around her shoulders adding to the heavy weight she was carrying as they walked along in silence. They only passed one other hardy soul braving the cold on the short jaunt to their local.

Gerry, the publican at the Four Horses, greeted them in his usual jocular manner and Bronagh went to sit at an empty table as far away from the door, to avoid the draft each time it opened, as she could find. She took her coat off and settled in her chair, toying with the beer mat as she waited for Kevin to return with their drinks and a packet of his customary Big D peanuts, despite not long having had his dinner. A pint wasn't a proper pint without a packet of peanuts, he'd maintain. A haze of smoke hung over the room and the traditional music was underway, several people clapping along and stamping their feet.

She'd have to shout to be heard, she thought, watching as Kevin weaved around the tables, the packet of peanuts tucked under his chin, a pint glass in one hand and her glass and bottle of Babycham in the other. He put her drink down in front of her and then took the packet out from under his chin, plopping the nuts down on the table. Lastly, he placed his pint glass down, before pulling the chair out and sinking into it.

'Is everything alright? You've been quiet since dinner,' he asked, leaning across the table to be heard.

'Not really. It wasn't Rhoda on the phone. It was Hilary.'

He raised an eyebrow over the top of his pint glass. He knew there wasn't much love lost between the sisters. 'Did she say something to upset you?'

'Only, Erin's got the flu, there's no question of Mammy going to Tramore for the weekend.' Her insides twisted at the unfairness of it. Why now? She knew she was being irrational; it wasn't Hilary's fault her daughter was sick but she'd been so looking forward to their weekend in Donegal and she couldn't possibly go now.

'I'm sorry, Kev,' her voice cracked, 'I'm not going to be able to go with you to Donegal. It's too short a notice to sort anyone else out to stay and I don't want to make a fuss about it because Mam will feel badly enough as it is.'

'You could leave her, it's only for a night or two. One of her friends or a neighbour could call in and check on her,' Kevin said, sitting back in his chair and running a finger around the rim of his pint.

'No,' Bronagh shook her head, wishing he wouldn't make this harder than it already was. 'It wouldn't be fair on Mam. She's used to someone else being in the house at night with her.

What if she got up in the night and fell? I couldn't live with myself.'

She had to strain to hear as Kevin said, 'But it was all arranged.'

'I know,' she took his hand. 'I was looking forward to it so much but Mam needs me. You know how it is, Kev.'

His expression was sulky and Bronagh dropped his hand feeling a frisson of annoyance penetrate her despondent mood. He was behaving childishly because he did know how it was, he'd known it right from the start. She wasn't free to come and go and she didn't mind because she loved her mam. Things were what they were. She and her mam, they were a team and they came as a package deal. She leaned back in her chair and focused on the band playing in the corner of the pub grateful their music meant she didn't have to try and jolly things along by making conversation.

When Kevin kissed her good night after walking her home later that evening, Bronagh detected a cooling between them that hadn't been there before.

Chapter 35

'MAUREEN, YOU LOOK WONDERFUL, sure you re-mind me of—' Donal said.

'Loretta Lyn.' Maureen supplied for him preening in her lacy yellow, nipped-in-waist dress.

'Exactly what I was going to say.'

He leaned in to kiss her and she turned her head at the last minute so his lips landed on her cheek. 'I can't have lipstick all over my face, Donal,' she said. 'Not when I'm going to be per-forming shortly.'

'Fair play to you but what about after you've performed?' He winked.

She giggled, girlishly. Donal had that effect on her.

'Before we go, I've something for you.'

'Oh yes?' She hadn't noticed his hands were behind his back and she waited to see what he was hiding.

He produced a tambourine and Maureen gasped because it wasn't at all like the one, she'd been rattling at Maria's these last few weeks. Oh no, this was a top of the line tambourine. Sure, it was the sort Stevie Nicks herself would be proud to get her hands on. It was white and gold and the nicest thing she'd ever been given, engagement and wedding band aside. 'I love it,' she breathed, eager to take it from him to give it a few shakes. The sound was warm and cutting.

Donal beamed. 'It's got nickel plated and brass jingles and the shape's designed for natural arm and hand motions.'

'I love it,' she reiterated.

'I thought you could use it tonight so you can be part of the whole set instead of just the two duets.'

'Do the lads not mind?'

'No, they think it's a grand idea, but they will mind if we don't get on the road. Are you ready?'

'Let me get my hat and I'm good to go.'

Maureen was fidgety with excitement as she rode in the van with Donal, who was driving, and the rest of the lads from The Gamblers whom she'd only met briefly once before. They were most accommodating and she could hear from the jokes being cracked in the back that they were all in good form. She could also tell they weren't used to having a lady along for the ride. Ah, well, at her age it'd take more than a ribald joke to make her blush. The tambourine was on her lap, jingling each time they went over a bump. Her hat, borrowed from Laura, was firmly in place and her new boots were squeezing her toes but she'd survive. There hadn't been a lot to choose from in the way of white cowboy boots, even in the city, and so she was stuck with a toe-pinching pair. She had the prime spot in the front passenger seat of the van next to Donal and whenever they were illuminated by a street light she'd admire the yellow sheen of her dress and resist the urge to pinch herself. She, Maureen O'Mara, was off to a party where she was going to be singing with the band. Sure, life could take some funny twists and turns. It was what made it so worthwhile, the not knowing what was around the corner and, just when you thought you'd hit a dead end, lo and behold a new road opened up.

The party was being held in a local rugby club which Donal located after only one wrong turn. He reversed the van up to the entrance so as they wouldn't have to lug their gear far. The car park only had a smattering of other vehicles in it; not surprising, given they were arriving an hour before the party was due to get underway in order to set up.

'You go on inside, Maureen,' Donal said. 'There's no need for you to be hanging about in the cold while we get organised.'

Maureen did as he'd suggested, pushing open the doors as though entering a saloon and venturing into the club rooms where the party was to be held. Bright red, blue, green and yellow clumps of balloons were dangling from the ceiling beams and a banner with 'Happy 70th Birthday Nora' was strewn across the top of the bar. Her nose was instantly hit with the stale smell of beer, cigarettes and sweat but overriding them was the far more alluring aroma of heating pastries. There was a fella behind the bar polishing glasses and he looked up upon hearing the doors open.

'You're a bit early, love,' he called over, doing a double-take as he registered her hat, boots and tambourine. Nobody had told him it was a country and western theme night. He'd have worn his bolo neck tie and sheriff's badge had he known. They hadn't had an outing since he'd gone to his Uncle Diarmuid's fiftieth birthday hoe down in Limerick. The craic had been mighty and the badge had worked wonders with the ladies. He grinned to himself recalling the fumble out the back he'd had with a lass in Daisy Duke denim shorts. Alright there wasn't much chance of her pasty white legs being insured for a million dollars but still, all in all it had been a memorable night. He glanced at the balloons remembering tonight was a seventieth birthday party and was suddenly glad he'd left his badge at home.

Maureen cleared her throat, gaining his attention once more, before saying the words she'd never thought to say in her lifetime, 'I'm with the band.' She tossed her head for effect and nearly lost her hat.

'The Gamblers?'

'That's them. I'm on percussion,' she shook her tambourine. 'And doing a couple of duets. The birthday girl's a fan of Sheena and Dolly.'

'I've heard they're good. I like a bit of Kenny Rogers now and again.'

'They are good,' Maureen said loyally, stepping aside to let Niall, the guitarist, who was toting a large amp past. He carried it over on bandy legs to the corner of the room where an area had been cleared of tables and chairs for the band and dancing. Davey followed with the keyboard and John who was on drums brought up the rear.

'A drink, lads? And lasses,' the bartender hastily added, catching Maureen's eye before doing the honours.

A pencil-like woman in a black fitted dress was next to arrive, along with her entourage of two children and a husband carrying an enormous cake. She directed him to the kitchen out the back, told the children to get themselves a lemonade, and made a beeline towards where Maureen and The Gamblers were supping their pints. They were enveloped in a cloud of thick, flowery perfume which made Maureen feel as though she were standing in a rose garden listening to a talking pencil.

'Hello there, I'm Patsy, the birthday girl's daughter.'

They returned the greeting and then she turned her attention to Donal. 'And you must be Kenny, I mean Donal. We talked on the phone.'

'We did.' Donal shook her hand.

'You're all set-up, I see.'

'We are, so you just give us the word and we'll start playing.'

'I thought we'd let everybody have a few drinks and catch up, something to eat that sorta thing, and then you could come on around nine. How does that sound?'

'Sounds grand.' He gave her a smile and she tottered off, waving over to a nattily dressed couple who'd appeared in the interim.

It wasn't long before a trickle of guests began arriving, milling about the room with exclamations of, 'I haven't seen you since Gina and Donald's wedding, it was a lovely roast dinner we were after having at the reception' or 'do you remember the holy show of herself Nancy made at Catriona's twenty-first doing the cancan, don't let her touch any top shelf drinks or she'll be flicking her skirt up at all and sundry,' and the like.

Maureen sat at the table along with the rest of the band, sipping her drink, watching the proceedings. Everybody was enjoying the craic and by the time she was on her second drink the tables were full and a small crowd was gathered near the bar, making the most of the tab. Conversation had been turned up a notch as drinks were consumed. The pencil-like woman with her hair scraped back in a bun was having no luck trying to get the party-goers to quieten down so as she could make an announcement. She enlisted Donal's help after several attempts and he switched on his microphone, handing it to her. Everybody froze as it screeched into life, fingers down a blackboard style, and then her voice boomed out. Donal had to whisper in her ear that it wasn't a good idea to hold your mouth right to the microphone and shout. Eventually, to everyone's relief, she found a happy medium and announced the birthday girl was two minutes away.

She'd only just conveyed her message when the doors burst open to reveal a sprightly woman with lots of glittery jewellery who was on the arm of a man whose silver-topped head was barely visible above the dinner jacket swamping him. An almighty cheer went up followed by shouts of 'Happy Birthday!' and some halfwit, eejit calling out, 'You don't look a day over seventy, Nora!'

The drinks flowed once more and yer man behind the bar deserved a medal for keeping up with the orders being shouted at him. Two youngsters, probably Nora's grandchildren, Maureen surmised, began doing the rounds of the room with platters of savouries and little triangle ham and egg sandwiches. It would take more than a sausage roll and a bite-sized sandwich to sort this lot out, Maureen mused, helping herself to a sausage roll. Only the one mind because she wasn't a hypocrite. Joan Fairbrother sprang to mind; she'd have cleared a tray up on her own given the chance.

As the evening wore on so too did Maureen's nerves. She'd have been grand if they'd gotten straight into it but the waiting around was giving her plenty of time to wonder what she was doing. Donal could see her leg jiggling and picked up on her nerves. He reached over and patted her knee giving her a reassuring smile. 'It's only another ten minutes and we're up. The trick is to pretend they're all naked, the lot of them.' He winked.

Maureen looked around the room and as her eyes raked over a portly chap, she was assailed by an image she hastily erased. 'If it's alright with you, I think I'll leave their under-

pants on,' she said to Donal, causing him to let out a loud guf-
faw.

'You do what works for you, Maureen.'

At last it was time for them to get up and the lads arranged
themselves with practised ease. Maureen took her place over
to the right of Donal, her new tambourine firmly in her grasp.
She willed her trembling hands to stay still and as the band
launched into *Reuben James*, Maureen forgot she was nervous
as she tapped the tambourine against her side and swayed to
the familiar rhythms. People began migrating toward the area
reserved for dancing in front of where they were playing and as
she saw enjoyment on their faces her confidence grew. By the
time the third song in the set came to a close she was relaxed
and having fun, as were the audience. Each song had been met
with loud applause. Donal paused between songs to introduce
her.

'We've a special guest joining The Gambler's tonight, Maureen O'Mara.'

Maureen basked in the applause.

'And isn't she pretty as picture?'

Some old letch with glasses so thick they could have been
cut off the bottom of milk bottles whistled. Maureen shot him
a look telling him to behave himself.

'A little bird told me that this is one of Nora, the birthday
girl's favourite songs. Happy birthday, Nora, this is for you.'
There was a loud whistle and a cheer went up quietening down
as the intro was played by Davey on the keyboard. Donal
crooned the opening lines and then Maureen leaped in, looking deep into his eyes as she sang, losing herself in Donal and
the music. She sang with every ounce of her being, she sang

from her heart, and as the number drew to a close the slow dancing couples broke apart to clap thunderously. It was a moment Maureen pressed like a flower between the pages of her mind to pull out in the years to come. She moved back to her post and was about to begin shaking her tambourine to *Daytime Friends* when she spied a face in the crowd. A familiar face whose mouth had formed an 'O' and catching her mammy's eye, Moira mouthed, 'Mammy, what the feck are you doing?'

For Maureen's part she wanted to know what Moira was doing at a seventieth birthday party at the Clontarf Rugby Club.

Chapter 36

IT WAS WHEN THE BIRTHDAY cake, a triple-layered cream sponge was being passed about the crowded and hot clubroom, Moira finally managed to pin her mammy down.

'Mammy, you should have told me.' Moira wasn't sure where to start with what exactly Mammy should have told her. That Donal was the lead singer in a Kenny Roger's tribute band? The penny had dropped as to who he'd reminded her of. It wasn't Father Christmas after all, it was Kenny Rogers. And then, there was the fact that Mammy was after playing tambourine in that band. Or, was it that she was doing a Kenny, Sheena duet? That she had white cowboy boots which were kind of cool, just not on Mammy? And, why was she wearing a yellow dress that could have served as a bridesmaid's dress in the seventies? Her mind was so full of all these questions jostling for attention she couldn't articulate any of them. 'I'm shocked, so I am.' Was all she could come up with.

'What are you doing here, Moira, are you following me?' Maureen narrowed her eyes.

Moira snorted. 'Mammy, I have better things to do than sneak after you on a Saturday night to see what you're getting up to. I'm here with Tom, it's his great aunt's birthday.'

Jaysus wept, but Ireland was a small country, Dublin an even smaller city; you could get away with nothing, Maureen mused.

'Moira!' Donal boomed, 'Fancy meeting you here.'

218

'Fancy,' Moira replied as Tom came up and joined her.

'Maureen, who'd have thought? You're a sly old dog.' Tom flushed realising what he'd said. 'What I meant to say was I didn't know you could sing. You were great so you were. It was like watching an episode of Stars in their Eyes.' He held out a hand to Donal. 'I'm Moira's fella, Tom, you must be Donal.'

Moira put a hand firmly on Tom's bottom as she spied two women around her own age giving him the glad eye. It was a momentary distraction from the whole Mammy, Sheena thing. He jumped at the unexpected bodily contact as he shook hands with Donal. 'You had everybody up on their feet,' he said, reverting to his normal height as Moira released her grip, satisfied she'd made her point. Still, she kept a firm eye on the two women as they mooched off to check out what other talent was on offer. Tom engaged Donal in a conversation about Shay, Roisin's boyfriend, who was also in a band while Maureen and Moira squared off.

'You've been keeping a lot of secrets, Mammy. Relationships are built on trust you know.'

Maureen frowned because she was certain she'd said those very words to Moira when she was younger. Yes, she could recall quite clearly her response to her youngest daughter telling her she was going to a church youth group club when in actual fact she'd been spotted by Aisling who hadn't hesitated to land her little sister in it, at the Hairy Lemon pub.

'I've been keeping secrets for a reason because you've far too much to say for yourself. Sure, if you'd known I was going to be here tonight with Donal and the band, you'd have poked fun at me and him.'

Moira would have liked to have said it wasn't true and she'd have done no such thing but she had an inkling it was exactly what she'd have done. Mammy had a point.

'It was a shock seeing you up there like that, is all. It's not every day your mammy, who only ever sang along to the radio gets up and sings Sheena Easton. I had no idea Donal was even in a band let alone a Kenny Roger's tribute band. He's very good,' she admitted, and then seeing her mammy's face added, 'And so were you. That's a grand tambourine you're after shaking and you hit those high notes like Sheena herself.' Moira was grateful Mammy was in the yellow dress and not the white, disco spandex pants Sheena had worn back in the day.

'Thank you, Moira, that's kind of you to say. I'm Dolly in the next set.' Maureen decided to be magnanimous too, although she knew her phone would be ringing first thing tomorrow morning with Aisling and Roisin demanding to know why she hadn't told them her new fella sang in a Kenny Rogers tribute band and how she was after singing Sheena at a seventieth birthday party. She wondered what they'd have to say when she told them she and Donal were talking about going to Los Angeles for a holiday to see Patrick. Plenty, she was sure, but she'd have to wait and see because for now her audience was waiting.

Chapter 37

1971

THE WEEKEND BRONAGH was supposed to have been in Donegal was the slowest one she'd ever known. She'd tried to quash the unease she felt at the memory of the last kiss she'd shared with Kevin and somehow, managed to keep a bright face on things for her mam's sake. 'Sure, there'll be plenty more times to go to Donegal. His family's not going anywhere, Mam, and as soon as Erin's well we'll sort out another date for you to go to Tramore. It's one of those things, what can you do?' she'd said, injecting a cheeriness she didn't feel into her voice.

Mam had been so disappointed she was going to miss out on seeing Hilary and the children. She'd been quiet all weekend, busying her hands with a tapestry of kittens playing with a ball of string she was working on for Erin's bedroom. Bronagh couldn't bear it if she felt guilty about her and Kevin's Donegal jaunt being cancelled too. She never wanted her to feel she was a burden because she wasn't. Truth be told, and it was something she'd only admit to herself, no one else, she needed her mam, just as much as Myrna needed her. She'd never lived anywhere but here and as time wore on, she found it hard to imagine living anywhere else.

Monday eventually crept around and Bronagh's day at work was a busy and welcome distraction to the waiting to hear from Kevin. A large, boisterous group of chemists from around the country had barrelled in on a group booking for a conference being held on Tuesday in the city. The day sped by and she was surprised and happy when she left O'Mara's late that afternoon to see Kevin waving out from across the road by St Fusilier's Arch. She waited for a break in the slow-moving traffic and ran over to where he was waiting with his hands shoved in the pockets of his leather jacket.

She wished she hadn't taken the gorgeous burgundy coat back now. It would have been nice to show it off to him. To put this missed weekend behind them. In a fit of martyrdom on Saturday morning though, she'd returned it to Brown Thomas. Now, all she wanted was to feel the reassurance of his arms around her and to rest her head on his shoulder so as to breathe in the familiar smoky, leathery smell of his jacket. Everything would be alright, she told herself, her face breaking into a wide, happy smile as she reached him. Just as she'd said to Mam, there'd be other opportunities for them to head north. 'Did you have a nice time?' she asked once she'd caught her breath.

'I did. It was good to see everybody and it gave me a chance to clear my head and think things through properly.'

'Oh.' There was a stiffness to his shoulders and she wondered whether he'd had a bad day at work. She knew he wasn't a fan of Mondays. Instead of the warm hug she'd anticipated she received a kiss on her cheek, his lips cool and dry as they grazed her skin and his expression unreadable. She stamped on the sick feeling in the pit of her stomach, telling herself she was a pessimist of the highest order. Everything would be alright. He was here, wasn't he? She didn't ask what things he'd needed to think through because she didn't want to know the answer.

He fished a packet of cigarettes from his pocket and tapped the pack, taking one and sticking it in his mouth. Bronagh watched as he lit it with the Zippo, the flame strong and steady despite the breeze. She tried to summon up the warm, happy emotions she'd felt lying next to him on the blanket that summer's day in Phoenix Park but they refused to come. Instead, she watched him inhale the smoke deeply before blowing it out to join the exhaust fumes from the passing cars. 'Shall we go for a walk?' He inclined his head toward the Green.

'Grand, it'll be good to stretch my legs after sitting down all day,' Bronagh replied with a brightness she didn't feel. She linked her arm through his and they walked through the arch and into the park where people, rugged up in their coats and hats, scurried past, not pausing to take in their surrounds in their eagerness to get home. Kevin smoked steadily and she walked beside him in silence and when his words came, they sounded harsh and overly loud as each one sliced through her.

'Bronagh, I think it's for the best if we stop seeing one another.' Kevin dropped the smouldering butt on to the ground grinding it out with the toe of his shoe.

She released her arm from his and stopped dead on the path, staring at him in disbelief, but he wouldn't meet her gaze. 'What are you talking about, sure, we're grand.' Her voice had a wavering pitch and Kevin glanced around nervously not wanting a scene. He pulled her toward a bench out of the way of the passing foot traffic and she sat down glad to take the weight off her feet because her legs were shaky, as was the rest of her body. He perched next to her leaning forward, leg jiggling, hands clasped, being sure to keep a careful distance between them.

Bronagh turned and saw his jaw set in a hard line. *This couldn't be happening!* 'Why, where's this come from? We were fine before you went home,' she managed to ask. Her hand reached out to rest on his arm pleading to understand.

'I wasn't fine, Bronagh, but Mam—'

'Oh, it's down to your mam, is it? Well, I don't see how she can have a say given she's never met me. That's hardly fair.'

'Listen, Bronagh.' His voice was hard. 'You didn't give her the chance to meet you and she only confirmed in my mind what I was beginning to feel anyway. I'm never going to come first with you.'

'What are you talking about?' She wished he'd stop jiggling his leg.

'With you, I'm never going to come first. I think you're as dependant on your mam as she is on you and she'll always be your first priority.' He looked at her now, daring her to say this wasn't the case.

'She's ill, Kev, c'mon you know that. She needs me.'

'Not you exclusively, Bronagh. There're others who'd be happy to help if you asked. Only you won't because you don't trust anyone else.'

'Oh no you don't. You can't put this all on me. I would have gone if Mam could've gone to Hilary's but, and through no fault of my own, she couldn't. You knew that.' Her voice wobbled dangerously at the unfairness of what he was saying and her eyes burned hot.

He shrugged. 'Either way, I don't want to be the third wheel.'

'How can you say that? You know you're not. I love you and Mam loves you too for that matter. She'd be heartbroken if she were privy to this conversation.'

Kevin licked his bottom lip. 'Bronagh, I've said my piece. It's how I feel. I won't change my mind and there's something else.'

'What?' Jaysus Christ what more could there possibly be?

'I gave notice at work today. I'm moving back to Donegal. There's a job opening for me there. I miss my family and there's no chance of you ever moving there with me. So, you see, it's easier to part ways now.' He shrugged again.

Fury at the way things had spiralled out of her control ripped through her and she stood up spitting out, 'Well go then. Good riddance,' before she walked away from him quickly, not wanting him to see the tears that were blinding her. She needed to get home to her mam.

Chapter 38

Present

THE DOOR TO THE GUESTHOUSE opened five minutes before Bronagh was due to head home and, looking up from where she'd been tidying her day's work away, she registered one of two things. An enormous box and a familiar face. She watched as the unexpected guest who was doing his best to balance the box with one hand and his case in the other beamed at her. She blinked rapidly because she'd already decided she must be seeing things. Surely she'd conjured him up because it couldn't be, but when she heard the apparition speak in a Liverpudlian brogue with a dash of Irish, she knew this dapper vision was real.

'Hello, Bronagh, I couldn't wait until September to try the carrot cake. It's far too far away, so here I am.'

Bronagh, mouth agape, put down the papers she'd been about to clip into a folder and got to her feet, her brain shuffling to arrange a coherent sentence. 'Leonard? What on earth are you doing here?'

'I've brought my annual visit to my fair city forward.'

'But I never saw your booking.' Bronagh was still agog, not registering what he was telling her.

'Will you let me put this down, woman?' He moved toward her, the box beginning to wobble precariously in his tenuous grasp.

'Of course. Here.' She hastily swept aside the folder, stapler and diary to make room on her desk and Leonard heaved a sigh of relief, placing the box safely down.

'That's better. Who'd have thought there'd be so much weight in it?' He doffed his hat at her, then taking it off kept it in his hand by his side as he smiled appreciatively. 'You're a sight for sore eyes, Bronagh. It's lovely to see you again.'

Bronagh's gaze flitted from him to the box and back again. Her mind was buzzing and she wasn't making sense of what he was saying. He'd come all this way to try the carrot cake? The man was mad.

He read her expression. 'I'm not mad. I wanted to surprise you and I can tell I've succeeded.' He looked thoroughly pleased with himself.

'You have.'

'A good surprise, I hope.'

'It depends on whether it's a carrot cake you've got in that box there.'

'But of course it is, and there's been a change of plan. I know I said I'd take you to Cherry on Top and treat you to a slice along with a cup of coffee but we've plenty of time over the next fortnight to do that. Besides, a whole cake has got to be better than a wedge and I thought your mum would appreciate trying a piece for herself.'

Bronagh's heart swelled at his thoughtfulness. Fancy him thinking of her mam, like that. She realised he'd said he was here for a fortnight. 'But where are you staying, and what about Bessie? I've not seen any booking for you here.' She opened her reservation folder and scanned the day's bookings. His name was definitely not there. She'd hate to disappoint him if he'd come over on a whim because they had a full house tonight.

'Well you won't find me registered under my name because that would've given away the surprise. I think you'll find my usual room has been booked under the name of Harry Bradshaw. He's looking after Bessie for me and she'll be spoiled rotten if I know Harry.'

'And who's Harry Bradshaw when he's at home?'

'My bowls partner.'

'Aha.' She'd grown fond of Bessie even though she'd never met Leonard's dog. She was pleased she was being well looked after. And does your sister know you've come to see her or is she in for a surprise too?'

'It's not my sister I've come to see.'

Bronagh flushed, feeling giddy as Leonard held his gaze steady with hers. He looked so handsome in his gentlemanly suit and tie.

Aisling broke the spell. 'Mr Walsh,' she clapped her hands delightedly. 'How wonderful to see you again. I didn't know you were coming! Bronagh, I never saw the booking? You should have told me one of my favourite guests was coming.'

'You wouldn't have seen the booking because he used an alias. And if I'd known, I would have told you. He's brought cake.'

'An alias?' Aisling was puzzled as to what was going on. She did like the sound of cake though.

Leonard stepped in, not offering an explanation as he said, 'I hear congratulations are in order, Aisling.'

'Yes, I'm a married woman, so I am. To Quinn from Quinn's bistro on Baggot Street.'

'I know the place. He's a fine chef your husband. I've dined there many a time and enjoyed the hearty fare. It's food served just as it should be. In fact, I've a booking there tonight for two.'

'Oh, are you taking your sister? I'll be sure to tell Quinn to keep an eye out for you to say hello.'

'No, not my sister. I'm hoping Bronagh will agree to joining me.'

Bronagh went puce as Aisling's raised-eyebrow gaze settled on her. O'Mara's receptionist had some explaining to do.

'We've been writing to one another, haven't we, Leonard,' she offered up.

'We have and the high spot of my week those letters from you have become too, Bronagh. It began when she sent me a Christmas card this Christmas just been. It was a lovely surprise and I sent Bronagh a card in return and the letters just fell in to place from there,' Leonard explained to Aisling.

Bronagh frowned. Hang on a minute. That wasn't right. 'No, Leonard, it was you sent me the Christmas card first.'

They both turned their bewildered expressions on Aisling who had a sheepish air about her as she looked everywhere but at them.

'It was you sent the card,' Leonard said and then he chortled and shook his head. 'Well, I never. I suppose I should say thank you.'

'It's a guesthouse you're after running not the Lisdoonvarna Matchmaking Festival,' Bronagh muttered but she couldn't be mad. Look what had happened since.

'Will I still be allowed a piece of cake?' Aisling asked, looking from one to the other.

'I suppose so,' Bronagh said.

'You didn't say whether you were free to join me tonight for dinner, Bronagh,' Leonard said, looking at her with hopeful expectancy.

She ignored Aisling mouthing 'say yes' as she pondered what she could organise for her mam's tea if she wasn't going to be home. Then, she pulled herself up sharply. She'd not make the same mistake twice. Mam would be fine. She was perfectly capable of doing herself something simple. Sure, there was nothing wrong with egg on toast now and again. 'I'd like that very much, Leonard,' she said sensing she'd just said yes to more than dinner. She'd said yes to a different, and brighter future than the one she'd thought lay in store for her. There was plenty of time to ponder what might be on the road ahead for her and Leonard Walsh, though. For now, it was time for a slice of carrot cake.

***Hi! I hope this latest instalment in The Guesthouse on the Green series made you smile, or even better laugh out loud which is something we all need during this tough time If you enjoyed Maureen and Bronagh's stories then leaving a short review on Amazon to say so would be wonderful and so appreciated. You can keep up to date with news regarding this series via my newsletter (I promise not to bombard you!) by subscribing via my website – www.michellevernalbooks.com[1] and to say thanks, you receive an exclusive O'Mara women character profile.

---

1.   http://www.michellevernalbooks.com

Book 8, The Guesthouse on the Green Series

The O'Mara's in LaLa Land

Pre-order available - Release date: 30 August 2020

READ ON TO FIND OUT about my new standalone novel, The Dancer – Pre-order available - Release date: May 31, 2020

The girl who used to dance like nobody was watching, vanished a long time ago...

For Veronica, her midlife crisis feels as if she's trapped in a deflating balloon. She's separated, works full time, has teenage sons whose moods fluctuate like the tides and, her mother, Margo, has early onset Alzheimer's and, unbeknown to Veronica, she's keeping a secret.

Veronica visits her mother twice a week at the care home where she resides, bringing in the costumes she wore as a young dancer when her future was bright and full of romance. As she talks about the past, she transports them back to that place in time before everything changed and she lost the love of her life.

But with Margo's memory disappearing has Veronica left it too late to tell her the part of her story they never talked about? If she has, then how can she ever heal from the events that derailed her life twenty-six years ago? And will Margo's lie shatter what Veronica's held on to as the truth for so many years.

On the Isle of Wight, Isabel's the girl with mermaid hair who'd lost her way until she found a place to call home on the island. She holds the key to giving Veronica's story a happy ending. But will the stars align and give her the strength she needs to reach out and find the part of her that's missing? And in doing so, will she hurt those she cares most about?

Printed in Great Britain
by Amazon